His gaze was dark with yearning, smoky with desire, and in that instant she lost herself, caught up in the flow of that heated current.

Caitlin needed his strength right then, his powerful arms around her—everything that meant shelter and protection from the outside world. She ran her fingers up over his chest, laced them around the strong column of his neck.

His kiss was gentle, coaxing, a slow, glorious exploration of everything she had to offer. His lips brushed hers, the tip of his tongue lightly, briefly tracing the full curve of her mouth, seeking her response. She kissed him in return, and in a feverish surge of passion he drew her close, easing her into the welcoming warmth of his taut, muscular thighs.

Her soft curves meshed with his hard, masculine frame and a ragged sigh escaped her, breaking in her throat. He kissed her thoroughly, desperately, his hands moving over her in an awed, almost reverent journey of discovery.

'Brodie…' She didn't know what she wanted to say…just his name was enough. She wanted him, needed him, longed for him to make her his.

Dear Reader,

First love, young love…such an intense, wonderful experience. Is it possible that it can survive the ravages of time and be a 'forever' kind of love?

Well, the answer to that is *maybe*. Sometimes it needs to change and mature, to grow into something else before young lovers can reach the fulfilment they long for.

Life in general—along with a broken romance and a troublesome background of family secrets—manages to get in the way and mess things up for Caitlin and Brodie when they meet up again in the beautiful surroundings of rural Buckinghamshire.

I hope you enjoy reading about their skirmishes and triumphs as they find one another once more.

With love

Joanna

RESISTING
HER REBEL DOC

BY
JOANNA NEIL

First published in Great Britain 2015
by Mills & Boon, an imprint of Harlequin (UK) Limited,
Eton House, 18-24 Paradise Road, Richmond, Surrey, TW9 1SR

© 2015 Joanna Neil

ISBN: 978-0-263-25863-9

Harlequin (UK) Limited's policy is to use papers that are natural,
renewable and recyclable products and made from wood grown in
sustainable forests. The logging and manufacturing processes conform
to the legal environmental regulations of the country of origin.

Printed and bound in Great Britain
by CPI Antony Rowe, Chippenham, Wiltshire

When **Joanna Neil** discovered Mills & Boon®, her lifelong addiction to reading crystallised into an exciting new career writing Mills & Boon® Medical Romance™. Her characters are probably the outcome of her varied lifestyle, which includes working as a clerk, typist, nurse and infant teacher. She enjoys dressmaking and cooking at her Leicestershire home. Her family includes a husband, son and daughter, an exuberant yellow Labrador and two slightly crazed cockatiels. She currently works with a team of tutors at her local education centre, to provide creative writing workshops for people interested in exploring their own writing ambitions.

CHAPTER ONE

'WHAT WILL YOU DO?' Molly stood by the desk at the nursing station, riffling through the papers in a wire tray. 'Will you go to the wedding?' She sent Caitlin a sympathetic glance. 'It must be a really difficult situation for you.'

Caitlin nodded. 'Yes, it is, to be honest. These last few weeks have been a nightmare. It's all come as a complete shock to me and right now I'm not sure how I'm going to deal with it.' She pulled a face, pushing back a couple of chestnut curls that had strayed on to her forehead. Her shoulder-length hair was a mass of wild, natural curls but for her work at the hospital she usually kept it pinned back out of the way. 'I don't want to go but I don't see how I can avoid it—when all's said and done, Jenny's my cousin. My family—my aunt, especially—will want me to be there for the celebrations. I don't want to be the cause of any breakdown in family relationships by not going. It will cause a huge upset if I stay away.'

Yet how could she bear to watch her cousin tie the knot with the man who just a short time ago had been the love of her life? She and Matt had even started to talk about getting engaged and then—*wham!*—Jenny had come along and suddenly everything had changed.

Her usually mobile mouth flattened into a straight line. When she'd opened the envelope first thing this morning back at the flat and taken out the beautifully embossed invitation card, her spirits had fallen to rock-bottom. She'd had a sick feeling that the day was headed from then on into a downward spiral.

Sure enough, just a few minutes later as she had opened the fridge door and taken out a carton of milk, her prediction was reinforced. She'd shaken the empty carton in disbelief. One of her flatmates must have drained the last drops of milk and then put it back on the shelf. She'd stared at it. No coffee before starting work? It was unthinkable!

'I can see how awkward it is for you.' Molly sighed, bringing Caitlin's thoughts back to the present. 'Families are everything, aren't they? Sometimes we have to do things we don't want to do in order to keep the peace. I just wish you weren't leaving us. I know how you feel about working alongside Jenny and Matt but we'll miss you so much.'

'I'll miss you too,' Caitlin said with feeling. Molly was a children's nurse, brilliant at her job and a good friend, but now, as Caitlin looked around the ward, she felt sadness growing deep inside her. She'd been working at this hospital for several years, specialising as a children's doctor, making friends and getting to know the inquisitive and endearing children who had come into her care.

It would be such a wrench to put it all behind her, but she knew she had to make a fresh start. She couldn't bear to stay while Matt was here. He had betrayed her and hurt her deeply. 'We'll keep in touch, won't we?' she said, putting on a bright face. 'I won't be going too far away—Buckinghamshire's only about an hour's drive from here.'

Molly nodded. She was a pretty girl with hazel eyes and dark, almost black hair cut in a neat, silky bob. 'Are you going to live at home? Didn't you say your mother needed to have someone close by her these days?'

'Yes, that's right. Actually, I thought it would be a good chance for me to keep an eye on her now that she's getting on a bit and beginning to get a few aches and pains. It's been worrying me for quite a while that I'm so far away.' She smiled. 'I think she's really quite pleased that I'll be staying with her for a while, just until I can sort out a place of my own.'

She started to look through the patients' charts that were neatly stacked on the desk. Her whole world was changing. She loved this job; she'd thought long and hard before giving in her notice, but how could she go on working here as long as Matt was going to be married to her cousin? And, worse, Jenny was going to take up a job here too.

She shuddered inwardly. It was still alien to her to think of him as her ex. They'd been together for eighteen months and it had been a terrible jolt to discover that he'd fallen out of love with her and gone off with another woman.

'I shall have to look for another job, of course, but

there are a couple of hospitals in the area. It shouldn't be too difficult to find something. I hope not, anyway.' She straightened up and made an effort to pull herself together. No matter how much she was hurting, she knew instinctively that it was important from now on to make plans and try to look on the positive side. She had to get over this and move on. She glanced at Molly. 'Perhaps we could meet up from time to time— we could go for a coffee together, or a meal, maybe?'

'Yeah, that'll be good.' Molly cheered up and began to glance through the list of young patients who were waiting to be seen. 'The test results are back on the little boy with the painful knee,' she pointed out helpfully. 'From the looks of things it's an infection.'

'Hmm.' Caitlin quickly scanned the laboratory form. 'It's what we thought. I'll arrange for the orthopaedic surgeon to drain the fluid from the joint and we'll start him on the specific antibiotic right away.' She wrote out a prescription and handed it to Molly.

'Thanks. I'll see to it.'

'Good.' Caitlin frowned. 'I'd like to follow up on him to see how he's doing, but I expect Matt will take over my patients when I leave here. I'll miss my little charges.'

Caitlin phoned the surgeon to set things in motion and then went to check up on a four-year-old patient who'd been admitted with breathing problems the previous day. The small child was sleeping, his breathing coming in short gasps, his cheeks chalky-pale against the white of the hospital pillows. He'd been so poorly when he'd been brought in yesterday and she'd been desperately concerned for him. But now, after she had listened to his chest and checked the monitors, she felt reassured.

'He seems to be doing much better,' she told his parents, who were sitting by his bedside, waiting anxiously. 'The intravenous steroids and nebuliser treatments have opened up his airways and made it easier for him to breathe. We'll keep him on those and on the oxygen for another day or so and you should gradually begin to see a great improvement. The chest X-ray didn't show anything untoward, so we can assume it was just flare-up of the asthma. I'll ask the nurse to talk to you to see if we can find ways of avoiding too many of those in the future.'

'Thank you, doctor.' They looked relieved, and after talking with them for a little while longer Caitlin left them, taking one last glance at the child before going back to the central desk to see if any more test results had come in.

'There's a phone call for you, Caitlin.' The clerk at the nurses' station held the receiver aloft as she approached the desk. 'Sounds urgent.'

'Okay, thanks.' Caitlin took the receiver from her and said in an even tone, 'Hello, this is Dr Braemar. How may I help?'

'Hi, Caitlin.' The deep male voice was warm and compelling in a way that was oddly, bone-meltingly familiar. 'I don't know if you remember me—it's been quite a while. I'm Brodie Driscoll. We used to live near one another in Ashley Vale?'

She drew in a quick breath. Brodie Driscoll! How

could she possibly forget him? He was the young man who had haunted her teenage dreams and sent hot thrills rocketing through her bloodstream. Just hearing his name had been enough to fire up all her senses. He had been constantly in her thoughts back then— and to be scrupulously honest even now the sound of his voice brought prickles of awareness shooting from the tips of her toes right up to her temples.

Not that she'd ever let on that he had the power to affect her like this—not then and certainly not now! Heaven forbid she should ever fall for the village bad boy, let alone become involved in any way with him. He was a rebel, through and through, trouble with a capital T... But who could resist him? His roguish smile and his easy charm made him utterly irresistible.

'Oh, I remember,' she said softly. She couldn't imagine why he was calling her like this, out of the blue. Not to talk about old times, surely? Her pulse quickened. Maybe that wouldn't be such a bad idea, after all...?

'That's good, I'm glad you haven't forgotten me.' There was a smile in his voice but his next words brought her out of her wistful reverie and swiftly back to the here and now. 'I'm sorry to ring you at work, Caitlin, but something's happened that I think you need to know about.'

'Oh? That's okay...what is it?' She'd no idea how or why he'd tracked her down, but he sounded serious, and all at once she was anxious to hear what he had to say.

'It's about your mother. I'm not sure if you know, but I moved into the house next door to hers a couple of weeks ago, so I see her quite often when she's out and about on the smallholding.'

She hadn't known that. Her mother was always busy with the animals and the orchard; knowing how friendly she was with everyone it was easy to see how she and Brodie would pass the time of day with one another. Her mouth curved. It was good that she had someone nearby to take an interest in her.

'What's happened?' she asked. 'Are the animals escaping on to your property?' Her mother could never resist taking in strays and wounded creatures and nursing them back to health. 'I know the fence was looking a bit rickety last time I was there. I made a few running repairs, but if there's a problem I'll make sure it's sorted.'

'No, it isn't that.' There was a sombre edge to his tone and Caitlin tensed, suddenly alert. 'I'm afraid it's much more serious,' he said. 'Your mother has had an accident, Caitlin. She had a fall and I'm pretty sure she's broken her hip. I called the ambulance a few minutes ago and the paramedics are transferring her into it right now. I'll go with her to the hospital, but I thought you should know what's happening.'

Caitlin's face paled rapidly. 'I— Yes, of course. I... Thank you, Brodie. I'll get over there... I need to be with her.' She frowned. 'What makes you think she's broken her hip?' She added tentatively, 'Perhaps it's not quite as serious as that.'

'That's what I was hoping, but she can't move her leg and it's at an odd angle—it looks as though it's become shorter than the other one. I'm afraid she's in a lot of pain.'

'Oh, dear.' Those were typical signs of a broken hip. The day was just going rapidly from bad to worse. 'Will they be taking her to Thame Valley Hospital?'

'That's right. She'll go straight to A&E for assessment.' He paused as someone at the other end of the line spoke to him. She guessed the paramedic had approached him to say they were ready to leave.

'I'm sorry, I have to go,' he said.

'All right...and thanks again for ringing me, Brodie.' She hesitated then said quickly, 'Give her my love, will you, and tell her I'll be with her as soon as I can?'

'I will.' He cut the call and Caitlin stood for a moment, staring into space, trying to absorb what he'd told her.

'Are you all right?' Emerging from one of the patients' bays, the senior registrar came over to the desk and looked her over briefly. 'You're as white as a sheet,' he commented. 'What's happened? Is it something to do with one of the patients?'

She shook her head. 'My mother's had an accident—a fall. A neighbour's going with her to the hospital—it sounds as though she's broken her hip.'

'I'm so sorry,' he said with a frown. 'I know how worrying that must be for you, especially with her not living close by. You'll want to go to her.'

'Yes, I do... But are you sure it's all right?' She wanted to jump at the chance to leave but she had patients who needed to be seen.

'It's fine. I'll take over your case load. Don't worry

about it. I'm sure Molly will fill me in on some of the details.'

'Thanks,' she said, relieved.

She left the hospital a short time later, walking out into warm sunshine. The balmy weather seemed so at odds with what was happening.

She picked up an overnight bag from her flat. The news was dreadful and she was full of apprehension about what she might find when she caught up with her mother. It was a relief at least to know that Brodie was with her. She must be in shock and in terrible pain but it would be a comfort to her to have someone by her side. Caitlin would be eternally grateful to Brodie for the way he had responded to her mother's predicament.

Guilt and anxiety washed over her. She should have been there; somehow she should have been able to prevent this from happening... She tried as best she could, but it wasn't always possible for her to get away every week, with shift changes and staff shortages and so on. It was frustrating.

Her heart was thumping heavily as she drove along the familiar route towards her home town. She had the car window wound down so that she could feel the breeze on her face, but even the heat and the beautiful landscape of the Buckinghamshire countryside couldn't distract her from her anxiety.

How bad was it? Being a doctor sometimes had its disadvantages—she knew all too well how dangerous a hip fracture could be, the complications involved: perhaps a significant amount of internal bleeding and the possibility of disabling consequences.

She gripped the steering wheel more firmly. Think positively, she reminded herself. Her mother was in good hands and she would be there with her in just a short time.

A few minutes later she slid the car into a parking bay at the Thame Valley Hospital and then hurried into the Accident and Emergency department, anxious to find out how her mother was getting on.

'They've been doing some pre-op procedures, X-rays and blood tests and so on,' the nurse said. 'And as soon as those are complete the surgeon will want to talk to her. Mr Driscoll thought maybe you might like to have a cup of coffee with him while you're waiting. He asked me to tell you he's in the cafeteria.' She smiled and added good-naturedly, 'If you leave me your phone number, I'll give you a ring when it's all right for you to see your mother.'

'Okay, thanks, that'll be great.' Caitlin wrote down her number on a slip of paper and then hurried away to find Brodie.

He caught her glance as soon as she entered the cafeteria. 'Hi there,' he said with a smile, coming to greet her, his blue gaze moving fleetingly over her slender figure. She had discarded the hospital scrubs she'd been wearing and had on slim, styled black jeans topped with a loose, pin-tucked shirt. 'It's good to see you, Caitlin.'

'You too.' Her voice was husky, her breath coming in short bursts after her rush to get here. That was the excuse she gave herself, but maybe the truth was that it was a shock to see Brodie in the flesh after all these years.

The good-looking, hot-headed youth she remembered of old was gone and in his place stood a man who simply turned her insides to molten lava. This man was strong, ruggedly hewn, his handsome features carved out of...adversity, she guessed, and...success? There was something about him that said he had fought to get where he was now and he wouldn't be giving any ground.

He was immaculately dressed in dark trousers that moulded his long legs and he wore a crisp linen shirt, the sleeves rolled back to reveal bronzed forearms. His hair was black, cut in a style that added a hint of devilishness to his chiselled good looks. Tall and broad-shouldered, his whole body was supple with lithe energy, his blue eyes drinking her in, his ready smile welcoming and enveloping her with warmth.

'Come and sit down,' he said, laying a hand gently on the small of her back and ushering her to a seat by the window. 'Let me get you a coffee—you must be ready for one after your journey.' He sent her a quick glance. 'I expect you've been told that your mother is having tests at the moment? The surgeon's going to see her soon to advise her about what needs to be done.'

She nodded. 'The nurse told me.' She sat down, her body stiff with tension. 'How is my mother?'

'She's okay,' he said cautiously. 'She's been conscious all the while, and the paramedics were with her very quickly after her fall, so that's all in her favour.'

'I suppose that's something, anyway.'

'Yes. The doctor who's looking after her gave her a pain-relief injection so she's comfortable at the moment. She's had an MRI scan to assess the extent of the injury—it's definitely a fracture of the hip, I'm afraid.'

She winced. 'Will the surgeon operate today, do you know?'

He nodded. 'Yes. I was told it will probably be later this afternoon—the sooner the better, in these cases. Luckily she hadn't had any breakfast to slow things up. You'll be able to see her before she goes to Theatre.'

'That's good.' She finally relaxed a little and when he saw that she was a bit more settled he left her momentarily to go and get her a coffee.

Caitlin glanced around the cafeteria. It was a large room, with light coming in from a wall made up entirely of windows. The decor was restful, in pastels of green and cream, and there were ferns placed at intervals, providing a touch of the outdoors.

Brodie came back to the table with a loaded tray and handed her a cup of coffee. It was freshly made, piping hot, and it smelled delicious. 'I thought you might like to try a flapjack,' he said, putting a plate in front of her. 'Something to raise your blood sugar a little—you're very pale.' He took a small jug and a bowl from the tray and slid them across the table towards her. 'Help yourself to cream and sugar.'

'Thanks.' She studied him thoughtfully. She couldn't imagine what it would be like having Brodie as a neighbour. 'How is it that you came to be living next door to my mother?' she asked.

He sat down opposite her. 'I'd been staying in a

room at the pub,' he said, 'while I looked around for something more permanent. Then the place came on the market as a suitable property for renovation. The old gentleman who owned it found the upkeep too much for him when his health failed. He went into a nursing home.'

'Lucky for you that the opportunity came your way,' she murmured.

He nodded. 'It's a substantial property—an investment project, possibly—and I thought it would be interesting to do up the house and sort out the land that goes along with it.'

'An investment project?' It didn't sound as though he was planning on staying around for too long once the place was renovated. 'Does it mean you might not be staying around long enough to make it a home?'

He shrugged negligently. 'I haven't really made up my mind. For the moment, I'm fed up with living in rented accommodation and wanted something I could renovate.'

'I see.' She picked up one of the golden-brown oatcakes and bit into it, savouring the taste. 'I didn't get to eat breakfast this morning,' she explained after a moment or two. 'Someone emptied the cupboards of cereals and bread.' She spooned brown-sugar crystals into her cup and sipped tentatively, all her regrets about missing the first coffee of the morning finally beginning to slip away. He watched her curiously.

'You were right,' she murmured at last. 'I needed that.' She told him about her flatmate drinking the last of the milk. 'It had to be Mike who was the culprit. Neither of the girls I share with would do something like that. He probably finished off the cornflakes as well.'

Brodie grinned. 'I guess he's down for a tongue lashing at some point.'

Her mouth twitched. 'Definitely, if only so I can vent…not that he'll take any notice. He never does—why should he when he leads a charmed life?' She took another sip of coffee. It was reviving and she savoured it for a moment or two before her thoughts shifted to her mother once more. 'Can you tell me anything about what happened this morning with my mother? I'm guessing you must have been outside with her when she fell.'

He nodded. 'I was about to head off for a meeting. Your mother usually feeds the hens first thing, and then checks up on the rabbits, and we say hello and chat for a minute or two. Today she seemed a bit preoccupied—she was worried a fox might have been sniffing around in the night—so she didn't say very much. She started to pull a few weeds out of the rockery and I went to my car. Then I heard a shout and when I looked around she had fallen on to the crazy paving. I think she must have lost her footing on the rocks and stumbled.'

Caitlin winced. 'I've told her to leave the rockery to me. I see to it whenever I'm over here. This is why I worry about leaving her on her own for too long. She's not so nimble on her feet these days, but she's always been independent, and if something needs doing she'll do it.'

'You can't be here all the time. You shouldn't blame yourself.'

She sighed. 'I do, though. I can't help it. I love her to bits and I often think I should never have taken the job in Hertford. It seemed like such a good opportunity at the time.'

He nodded agreement. 'Jane told me you're a children's doctor; she's always singing your praises. She's very proud of your achievements, you know.'

Caitlin smiled. 'She's always been the same. She sees the best in everyone.'

'Yeah.' Brodie gave a wry smile. 'She was the only one who ever saw any good in me. Of course, she'd been friends with my mother since they were at school together, so that must have helped.'

'Yes, I expect so.' Sadly, Brodie's mother had died in a car accident when he was a teenager. That was probably another reason why Jane Braemar had taken him under her wing. Caitlin had lost her father and there had been an immediate bond between her and Brodie because of their shared circumstances. They had each understood what the other had been going through, and in their own way had tried to comfort one another. It had given them a unique closeness, and it had also been good, a source of consolation, that her mother had looked out for Brodie in his darkest times. She'd stood by him all through his unruly, reckless phase.

She hadn't been able to do anything to stem the tide of hostility that had grown among the locals with Brodie's exploits, though.

After a whirlwind period of rebellion—of cocky, arrogant defiance, trespass, petty vandalism, and a 'love 'em and leave 'em' way with girls—even Brodie must have realised he'd gone too far and that he'd worn out any vestiges of goodwill people might have felt for a motherless boy. He'd finally used up all his chances. On his eighteenth birthday, his father had kicked him out of the family home and Brodie had had to hunt around for somewhere to live. He'd stayed with various friends, Caitlin recalled, before he'd left the village a year or so later. At the time, she'd been broken-hearted. She'd suddenly realised she didn't want him to leave.

Her phone trilled, breaking into her thoughts and bringing her sharply back to the present day. 'My mother's back on the ward,' she told Brodie after a second or two. 'The nurse said she's a bit drowsy from the pain medication but I can go and see her.'

'That's good. It might help to put your mind at rest if you can spend some time with her.'

She nodded. 'Thanks again for looking after her,' she said softly, her grey eyes filled with gratitude. 'I owe you.'

'You're welcome any time, Caitlin.' He stood up with her as she prepared to leave. He reached for her overnight bag. 'Let me help you with that,' he said.

'Thank you.' She watched him lift the heavy bag effortlessly. In it, she'd packed everything she thought she might need over the next few days, including her hairdryer, laptop, make-up bag and several changes of clothes.

'Have you thought about what will happen when your mother leaves hospital?' he asked as they set off for the orthopaedic ward. 'She'll need a lot of help with mobility. Perhaps she could go to a convalescent home for a few weeks?'

She shook her head. 'That won't be necessary. I'd planned on coming back to live in the village in the next week or so—this has just brought it forward, that's all.'

He frowned. 'You're leaving your job?'

'Yes. I'll have to find something else, of course, but I'd made up my mind that it was something I needed to do.'

'Are you doing this for your mother's sake or for some other reason?'

'A bit of both, really.' He was astute—she should have known that he would suspect an ulterior motive. 'I have some personal reasons for wanting to leave.'

'There wasn't a problem with the job, then?'

'Heavens, no.' She looked at him wide-eyed. 'I love my work. I just hope I can find something as satisfying to do here.'

They approached the lift bay. 'Hmm. Maybe I could help you out there,' he said. 'No promises, but I've just taken over as head of the children's unit here and I'm fairly sure I'll be able to find you a position.'

She stared at him in disbelief. 'You're a doctor?' Not only that, he was in charge of a unit. How could that be?

He nodded, his mouth quirking. 'I know that must seem strange, with my background, but thankfully I managed to get my head together before it was too late. I used a legacy from my grandfather to put myself through medical school. I didn't know anything about it until the lawyers contacted me but as far as I was concerned it came in the nick of time.'

She was stunned. 'I can't get used to the idea—you were an unruly, out-of-control teenager. You were always playing truant, going off with some friend or other to spend time in the woods.' She shook her head. 'Are you making this up?'

He laughed. 'No, it's all true. I took stock of myself one day and realised I was going nowhere fast. For all that I missed out on some of my schooling, I managed to get through the exams without too much bother, so when I made up my mind what I wanted to do it wasn't too difficult for me to get a place at medical school.'

They stepped inside the lift. 'What made you decide you wanted to be a doctor?' She still couldn't get her head around it.

His mouth flattened. 'I think my mother's accident had something to do with it, although I didn't consciously think of it in that way until some years later. I did some work with troubled teenagers and then I spent some time helping out in a children's home, supervising leisure activities and so on. I suppose that's what guided me towards a career working with young children. They aren't at all judgemental and I think that's what I liked most. They accept you for what you are; I find I can get along with them.'

The lift doors pinged and opened out on to the floor where the orthopaedic ward was housed. Brodie walked with her to the doors of the ward and then handed over her bag. 'I'll leave you to go and spend some time with your mother,' he said. 'Perhaps you'll think over what I said about the job? We always need paediatricians and even though I'm fairly new to the hospital I'm sure the bosses will accept my judgement on this.'

'I will give it some thought, of course—though I can't help thinking you're taking a bit of a risk offering me something like that when we've only just met up.'

'I suppose some might think that. Actually, though, I know your boss in Hertford. Jane told me you were part of his team and I knew then you must be good at your job. He's a decent man; he picks out good people.'

Her mouth curved. 'It sounds as though my mother has been giving you my life history.'

'Like I said, she thinks the world of you.' He scanned her face briefly. 'In fact, your boss actually mentioned you to me once. He said he had this dedicated young woman, Caity, working with him—though at the time I didn't realise he was talking about you.' He was thoughtful for a moment or two, then added, 'If you like, if you're stuck for something to do while your mother's in Theatre, you could maybe come over to the children's unit? The surgery will take a few hours and rather than you waiting about I could show you around. I'm on duty, but you could tag along with me, if that doesn't sound too off-putting?'

She nodded cautiously. 'It sounds fine to me. Perhaps I'll do that.'

He smiled then turned and walked away down the corridor. She watched him go. He was tall, straight backed and sure of himself. He'd always been that way, but whereas once there had been a brash recklessness about him it seemed to have been replaced with a confident, shrewd perception.

He'd made up his mind quickly about her and decided she would be capable of doing the job. She had accepted his explanation but perhaps his decision also had something to do with knowing her from years before.

She didn't know what to make of him. He seemed calm, capable, efficient and friendly—all good attributes. But could he really have changed so completely? Were there still vestiges from the past lurking in his character?

He was certainly impulsive. Was he still the same man who had girls clamouring for his attention? He'd enjoyed playing the field back then; he and his younger brother had caused havoc among the village girls.

She remembered one girl in particular, Beth, who'd been upset when Brodie had broken off their relationship.

He'd told her things were getting too heavy between them. He didn't want to settle down, wasn't looking for anything serious. He was still young and the world was his oyster. He wanted to get out there and explore what was on offer.

Caitlin frowned as she pushed open the door to the ward. What was she to think? Could she work with a man like that?

His personal life shouldn't matter to her, but she couldn't help wondering about him. Was he still the same man at heart—a man who could turn on the charm, make a girl desperate to be with him and then when someone more interesting came along simply cut things dead?

Wasn't that exactly what Matt had done to her when Jenny had arrived on the scene? It had hurt so badly to be treated that way. She had never thought it possible that he could do such a thing.

The truth was, she simply didn't trust men any more. From now on, she would keep her independence and wrap herself around in an impermeable, defensive coat to ward off any attempt to break her down and make her vulnerable again. That way, no one could hurt her.

Even so…she thought about what Brodie had said. A job was a job, after all, and that had to be top of her priorities right now, didn't it? She'd be a fool to turn down his offer, wouldn't she? Maybe she would talk it through with him in a while.

A small shiver ran through her. Right now, all these years later, he seemed like a good man, someone great to have around in a crisis, but you could never tell, could you? Agreeing to come and work with him would be a bit like making a date with the devil…albeit a devil in disguise, maybe. Would she come to regret it before too long?

CHAPTER TWO

'HOW ARE YOU FEELING, Mum? Are you in any pain?'
Caitlin sat by the bedside and reached for her mother's
hand, squeezing it gently. It upset her to see how pale
and drawn she looked.

'I'm okay, sweetheart. They gave me something for
the pain. You don't need to worry about me. I'm just
so glad to see you, but I'm sorry you were pulled away
from your work.' Her mother tried to stifle a yawn and
closed her eyes fleetingly. 'I don't know what's happening to me... I'm so tired.'

Caitlin smiled reassuringly. 'I expect there was a
sedative in the injection you had. The nurse told me it
won't be too long now before you go for your operation. That's good—they seem to be looking after you
really well. I'm very pleased about that.'

Her mother nodded, causing the soft brown waves of
her hair to flutter gently. 'They've all been so kind, explaining everything to me, telling me to take it easy and
saying how I shouldn't fret. I can't help it, though—
I keep thinking about the animals back home.' She
frowned and Caitlin could see that she was starting to

become agitated. 'They need to be fed and the crops have to be watered. It hasn't rained for a couple of days. With this warm, sunny weather everything will dry out.'

'I'll see to all of that,' Caitlin promised. 'You don't need to stress yourself about any of it. All you have to do is concentrate on getting better.'

'Oh, bless you—but there are so many things...' Her mother's brow creased with anxiety. 'You don't know about Ruffles' sores. He's the rabbit—someone brought him to me after they found him wandering in their garden.' She sighed. 'He needs a special lotion putting on his back. I should have collected it from the vet—I forgot to bring it home with me the other day. And the quail needs his claws clipping—he's another one a neighbour brought to me in a bit of a state. I was going to see to the clipping today—' She broke off, her breathing becoming laboured.

'It's all right, Mum,' Caitlin said in a soothing voice. 'Don't worry about it. I'll see to all of it and if anything else comes up I'll deal with that too.' She couldn't help but respect her mother for the way she coped with the smallholding, seeing to repairs, harvesting the crops and looking after various animals. Her mother had had a lot to cope with since she'd been widowed when Caitlin was a teenager, but she'd accepted the way things were, set to and got on with it. She was an incredible woman. 'Trust me,' Caitlin murmured. 'I just need to know that you're all right. Everything else will be fine.'

Her mother smiled wearily but she seemed comforted. 'I'm so glad you're home, Caity. I mean, I'm sorry for the reason for it—for this trouble with Matt, that must be so hard for you—but it'll be wonderful to have you close by.'

Caitlin patted her hand. 'Me too. I'm glad to be with you.' Even so, a faint shudder passed through her at the mention of Matt's name. She didn't want to think about him, and did her best to push him from her mind, but it was difficult.

She watched her mother drift in and out of sleep. It was worrying, not knowing how the surgery would go... It was a big operation... She'd already lost her father to a heart attack and she didn't want to lose her mother too.

She shook off those unreasonable fears. After the surgery her mother would need physiotherapy and would have to use crutches or a walker for some weeks or months.

'Oh, is she asleep?' A young porter came over to the bedside and spoke softly, giving Caitlin a friendly smile.

'She's drowsy, I think.'

'That's okay. It's for the best. It's time to take her to Theatre.'

Caitlin nodded and lightly stroked her mother's hair. 'I'll be here when you wake up,' she murmured, and the young man carefully wheeled his patient away.

'The operation could take up to three hours,' the nurse told her. 'You might want to take a walk outside, or go and get something to eat, if you don't want to go home. I can give you a ring when she's back in the recovery room, if you like?'

'Oh, thanks, that's really kind of you. I do appreciate it,' Caitlin said. She thought for a moment or two. What should she do? There might be time to go home. But perhaps she ought to follow up on Brodie's invitation… It was important that she found work quickly, though how she would manage her mother's day-to-day care when she was back home was another problem.

Decision made, she glanced at the nurse once more. 'Actually, I think I'll go over to the children's unit for a while. Dr Driscoll—the man who came in with her— said he'd show me around.'

'He's a doctor?' The girl's eyes widened. 'He must be new around here. I thought I knew most of the staff in the hospital. Wow! Things are looking up!'

Caitlin smiled. That was probably a fairly typical reaction from women where Brodie was concerned. He'd always turned heads. Perhaps she'd better get used to seeing that kind of response all over again. Of course, she knew how these women felt. Try as she might to resist him, she wasn't immune to his seductive charm.

She made her way to the children's unit, uneasily conscious of the quivering in her stomach now that she was to see him again. It was hard to say why he had this effect on her, but it had always been the same. There was something about him that jolted all her senses, spinning them into high alert the minute she set eyes on him.

The children's wards were on the ground floor of the hospital, a bright and appealing place with colourful walls, decorative ceiling tiles and amusing animal designs on the floor. There were exciting murals created to distract the children from the scariness of a hospital environment, and she noticed that the nurses were wearing patterned plastic aprons over their uniforms.

'Hi there.' The staff nurse came to greet her as she walked up to reception. 'I saw you admiring our wall paintings. They're very recent additions—Dr Driscoll brought in artists to do them the first week he started here.'

'Really?' Caitlin was astonished by that piece of news. 'My word, he doesn't let the grass grow under his feet, does he?'

'Too right. I heard he'd been talking with designers while he was working out his notice at his previous hospital. We all love the changes he's made. It's only been a few weeks and everything's so different here.' She paused by the entrance to the observation ward. 'You must be Caitlin,' she said with a smile. 'Am I right?'

'Well, yes…' Puzzled, Caitlin frowned. 'How did you know?'

The nurse's bright eyes sparkled. 'Dr Driscoll asked me to look out for you—he said I wouldn't be able to miss you. You had glorious hair, he said, beautiful auburn curls, and he told me what you were wearing. He's with a patient in Forest right now but he said to send you along.' Still smiling, she led the way. All the wards, Caitlin discovered, were divided into bays with names derived from the environment, like Forest, Lakeside, Beechwood.

'Ah, there you are,' Brodie murmured, looking

across the room, his mouth curving briefly as Caitlin entered the ward. 'I'm glad you could make it.'

She smiled in acknowledgment. He looked good, and the muscles in her midriff tightened involuntarily in response. He was half sitting on the bed. One long leg extended to the floor, the material of his trousers stretched tautly over his muscular thigh; the other leg was bent beneath him so as not to crowd out his small patient, a thin boy of around two years old.

'This lady is a doctor like me, Sammy. She's come to see how we're doing.'

Sammy didn't react. Instead, he lowered his head and remained silent, looking at the fresh plaster cast on his leg. Brodie sent him a quizzical glance. He silently indicated to Caitlin to take a seat by the bedside.

'His mother's with the nurse at the moment,' he said quietly. 'She's talking to her about the break in his leg bone and advising her on painkillers and so on.'

Caitlin nodded and went to sit down. She felt sorry for the little boy. With that injury perhaps it was no wonder the poor child didn't feel like responding.

Brodie turned his attention back to Sammy. 'Do you want to see my stethoscope?' he asked, showing it to the infant, letting him hold the instrument. 'If I put the disc on my chest, like this, I can hear noises through these earpieces…see?' He demonstrated, undoing a couple of buttons on his shirt and slipping the diaphragm through the opening. The little boy watched, his curiosity piqued in spite of his anxieties.

'Oh,' Brodie said, feigning surprise, 'I can hear a bump, bump, bump. Do you want to listen?'

The boy nodded, leaning forward to allow Brodie carefully to place the earpieces in his ears.

His eyes widened. Brodie moved the diaphragm around and said, 'Squeaks and gurgles, gurgles and squeaks. Do you want to listen to your chest?'

Sammy nodded slowly and, when Brodie carefully placed the disc on the boy's chest, the child listened, open-mouthed. He still wasn't talking but clearly he was intrigued.

'Do you think I could have a listen?' Brodie asked and he nodded.

Brodie ran the stethoscope over Sammy's chest once more. 'Hmm. Just like me, lots of funny squeaks and crackles,' he said after a while, folding the stethoscope and putting it in his pocket. 'Thanks, Sammy.' He picked up the boy's chart from the end of the bed and wrote something on it, getting to his feet and handing the folder to the nurse who was assisting.

A moment later, he glanced back at the child. 'The nurse will help you to put your shirt back on and then you can lie back and try to get some rest. Your mummy will be back soon. Okay?'

Sammy nodded.

Caitlin followed as Brodie walked away from the bed and spoke quietly to the nurse. 'There's some infection there, I think, so we'll start him on a broad-spectrum antibiotic and get an X-ray done. He's very thin and pale,' he added. 'I'm a bit concerned about his general health as well as the injury to his leg—I think we'll keep him in here under observation for a few days.'

'Okay.'

He left the room with Caitlin but at the door she turned and said quietly, 'Bye, Sammy.'

The infant looked at her shyly, not answering, and as they walked out into the corridor Brodie commented briefly, 'He seems to be very withdrawn. No one's been able to get a natural response from him.'

'How did he come to break his leg?'

'His parents said he fell from a climbing frame in the back garden. He'll be in plaster for a few weeks.' He frowned. 'The worry is, there was evidence of earlier fractures when we did X-rays. He was treated at another hospital for those, but the consultant there brought in a social worker.'

She looked at him in shock. 'Do you think it might be child abuse?'

'It's a possibility, and the fact that he's so quiet and withdrawn doesn't help. I'd prefer to make some more checks, though, before involving the police.'

She shook her head. 'I just can't imagine why anyone would hurt a child. It's unbearable.'

'Yes, it is. But Sammy's parents do seem caring, if a little naive, and at least he'll be safe here in the meantime.'

They went back to the main reception area and she tried to push the boy's plight to the back of her mind as Brodie began showing her around the unit. Each ward was set out in a series of small bays that clustered around a central point housing the nursing station. He stopped to check up on various patients as they went along.

'It's a beautifully designed children's unit,' she remarked some time later as they stopped off at the cafeteria to take a break for coffee.

'That's true,' he agreed, 'But I think there are things we can do to make it even better for the patients and their families. There are some children—like Sammy, perhaps—who need more than medicine and good nursing care to help them to get well. I want to do what I can to help them feel good about themselves.'

She sent him an oblique glance. 'That's a tall order,' she murmured, but perhaps if anyone could do it he could. He certainly seemed to have the determination to set things in motion. But then, he'd always had boundless energy and drive, even though he might have used it to the wrong ends years ago when he was a teenager.

'Well, if I'm to be any good at my job, I need to feel I'm making a difference,' he said. 'It's important to me.'

She studied him thoughtfully. He was an enigma—so focused, so different from the restless, cynical young man she had known before. 'That must be why you've come so far in such a short time. Your career obviously means a lot to you.'

'Yes, it does…very much so. I've always aimed at getting as far as I can up the ladder. I try to make all the improvements I can to a place where I work and then move on—at least, that's how it's been up to now.'

So he probably wouldn't be staying around here once he'd made his mark. She frowned. But this time he'd bought a house and he planned to do it up—would that make a difference to his plans? Probably not. Houses could be sold just as easily as they'd been bought.

He finished his coffee and then glanced at the watch on his wrist. 'I must go and look in on another young patient,' he murmured in a faintly apologetic tone.

'That's okay. I've enjoyed shadowing you, seeing how you work.'

He looked at her steadily. 'So, do you think you might want to work with us?'

She nodded. 'Yes—but only on a part-time basis to begin with, if that's possible. I'll need to be close at hand for my mother when she's back at home.'

He smiled. 'I can arrange that.'

'Good.' Her phone rang just then, and after listening for a while, she told him, 'My mother's in the recovery ward. I need to go and see how she's doing.'

'Of course.' He sent her a concerned glance. 'I hope she's all right. I know how worried you must be about her.' He went with her to the door of the recovery ward. 'Perhaps I'll see you later on, back at home?'

'I expect so.' She wasn't planning ahead, just taking one step at a time. It seemed like the best way to proceed at the moment. 'Thanks for showing me around, Brodie,' she said. 'Your children's unit is a really wonderful place and everyone involved with it is so dedicated. If children have to be in hospital, I think they're lucky to be here rather than in any other unit.'

'I'm glad you think so.' He smiled at her, pressing the buzzer to alert a nurse to release the door lock. 'It's been good meeting up with you again, Caitlin.' Somehow they had ended up standing close together, his arm brushing hers, and her whole body began to tingle in response. She didn't know how to cope with the strange feelings that suddenly overwhelmed her. It was bewildering, this effect he had on her. She loved Matt. How could she be experiencing these sensations around another man?

As soon as the door swung open she moved away from him, going into the ward. 'Thanks for coming with me and showing me the way,' she murmured, sending him a last, quick glance.

At last she could breathe more easily... But she hadn't been the only one to be affected by their momentary closeness to one another; she was sure of it. His awareness was heightened too. She'd seen it in his slight hesitation, the way his glance had lingered on her, and now she felt his gaze burning into her as she walked away from him.

How was it going to be, having Brodie living nearby? Part of her was apprehensive, worried about how things might turn out. After all, it was one thing to contemplate working with him, but having him as a neighbour could end up being much more than she'd bargained for.

She couldn't quite get a handle on what it was that bothered her about the situation, exactly. Over the last few weeks her world had been shaken to its foundations by the way Matt had behaved. She was unsettled, off-balance, totally out of sync. In her experience having Brodie close by could only add to her feelings of uncertainty. He was a spanner in the works, an unknown quantity.

She frowned. Perhaps the neighbour dilemma would only last for a short time, while her mother recovered from surgery. After that she could find a place of her own, away from Brodie, but near enough so that she could keep an eye on her mother and at the same time maintain her independence.

The nurse in charge of the recovery ward showed her to her mother's bedside. 'She's very drowsy, and unfortunately she's feeling nauseous, so it might be best for you to keep the visit short. She'll probably be more up to talking to you in the morning.'

Caitlin nodded. 'Okay.' She asked cautiously, 'Did the operation go well?'

'It did. The surgeon placed screws across the site of the fracture to hold everything in place and that all went quite satisfactorily. Your mother will need to stay in hospital for a few days, as you probably know, but we'll try to get her walking a few steps tomorrow. It seems very soon to get her on her feet, I know, but it's the best thing to do to get her on the mend.'

'All right. Thanks.' It was a relief to know that the major hurdle was over. Now the hard work of rehabilitation would begin.

Caitlin went to sit by her mother's bedside for a while but, as the nurse had said, she was very sleepy, feeling sick and wasn't up to saying very much. 'I'll leave you to get some rest, Mum,' Caitlin said after a while. 'I'll come back to see you tomorrow.'

She took a deep breath and left the hospital. At least her mother had come through the operation all right.

That was a huge relief. She could relax a little, now, knowing that she was being well looked after.

On the way home she called in at the vet's surgery to pick up the lotion that her mother had mentioned earlier.

'It's a mite infection,' the veterinary nurse told her after looking at the notes on the computer. 'You can't see the mites on the rabbit's skin, they're so tiny, but you might see dander being moved about.' She made a wry face. 'That's why the condition's sometimes known as "walking dandruff".'

Caitlin pulled a comical face at that, accepting the box containing the lotion that the nurse gave her.

'The vet gave Ruffles an injection,' the nurse said. 'But you need to put a few drops of the lotion on the back of his neck to get rid of any mites that are left. I think Mrs Braemar forgot to take it with her when she came here yesterday. He'll need another injection in eight days' time. Meanwhile, you could comb him to get rid of any loose fur and dander.'

'I'll do that. Thanks.'

Caitlin drove home through lanes lined with hedgerows, eventually passing over the bridge across the lock where brightly painted narrowboats were moored by the water's edge. Soon after that she came to a sleepy, picturesque village, a cluster of white-painted cottages with russet tiled roofs and adorned with vibrant hanging baskets spilling over with masses of flowers.

Her former family home was about half a mile further on, a rambling old house set back from the road, protected by an ancient low brick wall. There was one

neighbouring property—Brodie's—but otherwise the
two houses were surrounded by open countryside, giving them a magnificent view of the rolling hills of the
beautiful Chilterns.

Trees and flowering shrubs surrounded the front and
sides of her mother's house, adding glorious touches
of colour around a lush, green lawn. Caitlin gave a
gentle sigh of satisfaction. She always felt good when
she returned home. Here was one place where she felt
safe, sheltered.

Her old bedroom was just as she'd left it the last
time she'd been here, about three weeks ago, except
that her mother had laid a couple of books on her bedside table in readiness for her homecoming. Caitlin's
mouth flattened a little. That had been unexpectedly
brought forward by her mother's fall. She'd talked to
her boss about it and he'd said she could take compas-
sionate leave instead of working out her notice. It was
a relief to know she had no worries there, at least.

She went into the farmhouse kitchen and made herself a snack of homemade soup from a tureen she found
in the fridge, eating it with buttered bread rolls. The
soup was made from fresh vegetables that her mother
grew in the large kitchen garden out the back, and as
she ate it Caitlin was filled with nostalgia. She had
loved growing up here, having her friends to stay and
her cousins to visit.

It was sad, then, that her cousin Jenny should be the
one to steal the man she loved. Her fingers clenched
on the handle of her spoon. How could things have

turned out this way, leaving all her hopes and dreams cruelly shattered?

She pushed away her soup bowl and started to clear the table. Keeping busy was probably the best thing she could do right now. She made a start on various chores around the house, seeing to the laundry and collecting a few clothes and necessities to take into hospital for her mother. When she had done all she could in the house, she went outside to water the crops, and after that she made a start on the animal feeds.

True to form, as with everything that had happened so far today, she discovered from the outset things weren't going quite to plan. As she approached the hen house there was a sudden honking sound, an awful shrieking that made her cover her ears and look around to see what on earth was going on.

A trio of buff-coloured geese came rushing towards her, flapping their wings and cackling loudly. The male bird—she assumed he was male, from his aggressive manner—hissed at her and made angry, threatening gestures with his beak, while the other two kept up a noisy squawking.

'Go away! Shoo!' Her counter-attack made them stop for a second or two, but then the threats started all over again and she looked around in vain for a stick of some sort that she could wave at them. The way things were going, they weren't going to let her anywhere near the hen house.

'Get back! Shoo!' She tried again, frantically trying to keep them at bay for the next few minutes.

'Are you having trouble?' To her relief, she saw Brodie striding rapidly down the path towards her. Perhaps he would know how to stop the birds from attacking. 'I heard the racket they were making, so I came to see what's happening.'

'I don't think they want me around,' she said, concentrating her efforts on warding off the gander. 'In fact, I know they don't.'

'They're protecting their territory. Flap your arms at them and hiss back... You need to show them who's boss.'

She did as he suggested, waving her arms about and making a lot of noise. Brodie joined in, and to her amazement the geese began to back off. The gander— the male bird—was the last to give way, but eventually he too, saw that she meant business.

'Well done!' Brodie said approvingly when the birds had retreated. 'They're not usually an aggressive breed, but the males can be bullies sometimes, and you have to show them you're bigger and more fierce than they are. I'd say you've won that one!'

'Well, let's hope I don't have to go through that palaver every time I want to feed the hens. At least I'll be prepared next time.' She was breathing fast after her exertions and she was sure her cheeks must have a pink glow to them. 'I'd no idea Mum had bought some new birds.'

'She liked the idea of having goose eggs and thought the geese might sound a warning if any foxes came sniffing around.'

'Ah. I guess they're doing what she wanted, then. They're guarding the place.'

Perhaps he saw that she'd had enough of trouble for one day because he came up close to her and gently laid an arm around her shoulders. 'It hasn't been the best homecoming for you, has it? How about you finish up here and then come over to my place for a cold drink?'

'I…I don't know…' She was suddenly flustered, very conscious of his long body next to hers, yet at the same time strangely grateful for the warm comfort of his embrace.

He'd changed into casual chinos and a short-sleeved cotton shirt that revealed his strong biceps. The shirt was undone at the neck, giving a glimpse of his tanned throat.

'I…um…there's a lot to do; I still have to find the quail and clip his claws.' She pushed back the curls that clung damply to her forehead and cheek. 'I've never done it before, so it could take me a while to sort things out—once I manage to catch him, that is.'

'I can do that for you. He's in with the hens; your mother pointed him out to me a few days ago. She said wherever he came from, he hadn't been able to run around and scratch to keep his claws down, so that's why they need doing. It's not a problem. I know where she keeps the clippers.'

'Oh.' That would be a terrific help, one less problem for her to manage. 'Okay, then, if you're sure you don't mind?' Her excuses obviously weren't going to pass muster with him. Anyway, a cold drink was really, really tempting right now when she was all hot and bothered. She wiped her brow with the back of her hand.

'Good, that's settled, then. I do a great watermelon

and apple blend. I remember you used to like that.' He released her, but her skin flushed with heat all over again at the memory of hot summer days spent with her friends in flower-filled meadows.

Brodie and his brother had often come with them as they'd wandered aimlessly through the fields and by the river. They would stop to share sandwiches and drink juice or pop they'd brought with them. They had been fun days, days of laughter and innocent, stolen kisses in the time before Brodie had unexpectedly, disastrously, gone off the rails.

Together, they finished off the feeding then she watched as Brodie deftly caught the quail and carefully set about trimming the tip of each claw. 'These little birds get stressed easily,' he said, 'So it's best to get them used to being handled.' He placed him back down in the pen and the bird scampered off as fast as he could. 'He'll be all right now. I doubt he'll need clipping again now that he has a solid floor to run on and plenty of scratching litter.'

'Thanks for that.' Finished with all the chores for now, Caitlin locked up the pen and together they walked over to his house. It was a lovely big old property with a large, white-painted Georgian extension built on to an original Tudor dwelling. The walls were covered with rambling roses and at the side of the house there was an overgrown tree badly in need of pruning. The front lawn was dotted about with daisies and unkempt shrubs sprawled over the borders.

'I need to get the garden in order,' Brodie said ruefully, 'But I've had other priorities up to now, at work and back here.' He led the way along the path to the back of the house. 'In estate agent jargon, "in need of some renovation"; that can be interpreted in lots of ways,' he said with a wry smile.

She nodded, sharing the joke. 'I've always loved this house,' she said, glancing around. 'I expect it will need a lot of care and attention to restore it to its former glory, but it'll be worth it in the end.'

He nodded. 'I think so too. That's why I was so pleased when it came on to the market. I took to this house from a very early age. When I was about ten my friends and I used to climb over the wall and steal the apples from the orchard, until one day old Mr Martin caught us. We thought we were in big trouble, but he surprised us. He invited us into the house, gave us cookies and milk, then sent us on our way with a basket full of fruit.'

'He was a kind old man.'

'Yes, he was.' He showed her into the kitchen and she looked around in wonder.

'You've obviously been busy in here,' she said admiringly. 'This is all new, isn't it?'

'It is. It's the first room I worked on. I looked into different types of kitchen design and decided I wanted one where there was room for a table and chairs along with an island bar. This way, I can sit down for a meal and look out of the window at the garden; or if I'm feeling in a more casual mood, I can sit at the bar over there and have a cold drink or a coffee or whatever.'

She smiled. 'I like it, especially the cream colour scheme. You have really good taste.' She studied him afresh, surprised by the understated elegance of the room.

'Good taste for a rebel whose idea of fun was to spray graffiti on any accessible wall?' He laughed. 'I'll never forget that day you let rip at me for painting fire-breathing dragons on your mother's old barn. You handed me a brush and a pot of fence paint and told me to clean it up.'

'And you told me to forget it because the barn was old and rotting and ready to fall down—but later that night you came back and painted the lot.'

His brow lifted in mock incredulity. 'You mean, you've known all along who did it?'

She laughed. 'I never thought you were as bad as people said. I knew there was a good person struggling to get out from under all that bravado.' She'd understood him, up to a point, knowing how much it hurt to lose a parent. She'd turned her feelings inwards but back then Brodie had become more confrontational and forcefully masculine.

Smiling, he filled a blender with slices of apple and watermelon and added ice cubes to the mix. He topped that with the juice of a lime and then whizzed it up. 'That looks ready to me,' he said, eyeing the resulting juice with satisfaction. 'We'll take this outside, shall we?'

She nodded and followed him through the open French doors on to a paved terrace where they sat at a white wrought-iron table looking out on to a sweeping lawn. This was part of the garden that he had tended to, with established borders crowded out with flowering perennials, gorgeous pink blossoms of thrift with spiky green leaves alongside purple astilbe and bearded yellow iris.

He poured juice into a tall glass and handed it to her. 'I hope you still like this as much as you used to.'

She put the glass to her lips and sipped. 'Mmm... It's delicious,' she said. 'Thanks. I needed that.'

'So, what's been happening with you over the last few years?' he asked, leaning back in his chair and stretching out his long legs. He glanced at her ringless left hand. 'I heard you were dating my friend, Matt, until recently.'

She pulled a face, bracing herself to answer him. 'Yes, that's right. We were going to get engaged,' she said ruefully. 'But then things went wrong. Disastrously wrong.'

It was still difficult for her to talk about it but at the hospital where she had worked with Matt everyone knew the situation and it had been virtually impossible to escape from the questions and the sympathy.

He frowned. 'I'm sorry. Do you want to tell me what happened? Do you mind talking about it?'

'It still upsets me, yes.' She hesitated. 'He met someone else.'

Brodie studied her, his eyes darkening. 'I knew about that but I never understood how it came about. Matt and I haven't seen each other for quite a while. Was he looking to get out of the relationship?'

'No...at least, I don't think so.' She thought about it and then took a deep breath. 'It started about a year and a half ago. My cousin Jenny's car broke down one day and when Matt heard about it he offered to go and pick her up. Apparently she was in a bit of a state—she'd missed an appointment, everything had gone wrong and she was feeling pretty desperate. So he took her along to the nearest pub for a meal and a drink to give her time to calm down. Things just went on from there—he was hooked from that meeting. It was what you might call a whirlwind courtship.' She frowned. 'You knew Matt from school, didn't you? I suppose you know they're getting married soon?'

He sent her a cautious glance. 'I received an invitation to their wedding this morning.'

'Yes, so did I.'

'It was short notice, I thought. They must be in a hurry.' A line creased his brow. 'How do you feel about it?'

She exhaled slowly. 'Pretty awful, all things considered.' She picked up her glass and took a long swallow. The cold liquid was soothing, and she pressed the glass to her forehead to cool her down even more. 'They wanted to get married before the summer ends and the vicar managed to fit them in.'

He was thoughtful for a while. 'How are you going to cope with the wedding? Will you go to it? Yours has always been a tight-knit family, hasn't it? So I can see there might be problems if you stay away.'

'I don't know what to do. I feel hurt and upset. The thought of it makes me angry but, like you say, my family has always been close and if I don't go there could be all sorts of repercussions. I keep thinking maybe

I'll develop a convenient stomach bug or something on the day.'

He winced. 'I doubt you'll get away with that.'

'No.' She pulled a face. 'You're probably right.' She sighed. 'My mother's already upset because she might not be well enough to attend. Jenny's her sister's child. My mother and my aunt have always been very close. I suppose it all depends how well her recovery goes.'

'Let's hope it all goes smoothly for her.' On a cautious note, he asked quietly, 'Did Jenny know about you and Matt—about you being a couple? If she did, she must have known it would cause problems with your family.'

She shook her head. 'Not until it was too late. I was upset, devastated, but I tried to keep the peace for my aunt's sake and my mother's. But it's been hard, keeping up a pretence. I'm not sure how I'll get through the wedding without breaking down.'

She didn't know why she was opening up to him this way. It was embarrassing; she'd been humiliated and her pride had taken a huge blow. But Brodie was a good listener. He seemed to understand how she felt and she was pretty sure he wouldn't judge her and find her wanting.

'We could go to the wedding together,' he said unexpectedly. 'I'd be there to support you and we can put up a united front—show them that you don't care, that you're doing fine without him.'

'Do you think so? That would be good if it worked,' she said, giving him a faint smile. 'I'm not sure I could pull it off, though.'

'Sure you can. I'll help you. We'll make a good team, you and I, you'll see.'

She might have answered him, but just then a noise disturbed the quiet of the afternoon—the sound of footsteps on pavement—and a moment later Brodie's brother appeared around the back of the house.

'Hey there. I've been ringing the front doorbell but no one answered. I felt sure you were around some-where because I saw the car.' He glanced at Caitlin and did a double take. 'Hi, babe,' he said, his voice brim-ming over with enthusiasm. 'It's good to see you, Cait-lin. It's been a long time.'

'Yes, it has.' She was almost glad of the interrup-tion. Anything and anyone that could take her mind off Matt was welcome. 'Hi, David. How are you doing?'

He was a good-looking young man in his late twen-ties with dark hair, brown eyes and a lively expression. 'I didn't know you were living in our part of the world,' she said. 'I thought you were settled in London.'

'I am, mostly, but we're doing some filming down here for the latest episode in the TV drama series *Mur-der Mysteries*—I'll bet you've seen it, haven't you? It's been on the screens for over a year. It's turned out to be really popular, much more so than we expected.'

She nodded. 'I've seen it. It's good—you've cer-tainly found yourselves a winner there.' She studied him briefly. He too had come a long way in just a few years. 'I see your name on the credits quite often. So, am I right in thinking you write the screenplay?'

'I do.'

Brodie pulled out a chair for him and David sat

down. 'Do you want a drink?' Brodie asked, lifting the jug of juice.

'Sure.' He glanced at the pink liquid in the jug. 'It looks great, but is there a drop of something stronger you could put in it?'

'I can get you something from the bar if that's what you want.' Brodie sent him a thoughtful glance. 'Do I take it you're not planning on driving anywhere after this, then?'

David shook his head and sent Brodie a hopeful look. 'I was wondering if I might be able to stay here for the duration—while the research and the filming is going on.' He frowned, thinking it through. 'It could take several weeks, depending on what properties we need to rent, though the actual filming won't take more than a few days. Would that be all right?'

'Of course.' Brodie sent him a fleeting glance. 'You don't want to stay with Dad, then, at the Mill House?'

David sobered. 'Well, you know how it is. I love the old fellow but he's not much fun to be around lately. At least, not since…' He trailed off, his voice dwindling away as he thought better of what he was going to say.

'Not since he heard I was back in the village…is that what you were going to say?' Brodie made a wry smile. 'It's okay. I know how it is.' He pressed his lips together in a flat line. 'Things are still not right with us after all this time…' He shrugged. 'What can I do?' It was a rhetorical question. Caitlin sensed he didn't expect an answer. 'I've tried making my peace with him over the years, and again these last few weeks, but he doesn't seem to want to know. That's okay; I accept things as they are.'

Caitlin watched the emotions play across his face. Things had gone badly wrong between Brodie and his father and no one had ever known why. It had been the start of Brodie's resentment and rebellion; nothing had gone right for him for a long time after that.

'I'm sorry, Brodie,' David said. 'I'm sure he'll come around eventually.'

'Do you really think that's going to happen after all these years?' Brodie gave a short laugh. 'I wouldn't bet on it.'

'Maybe he'll get a knock on the head and develop amnesia. You'll be able to start over.' David grinned and Brodie's mouth curved at the absurdity of the situation.

'I guess we can see how you came to be a screenwriter, brother. You have a vivid imagination.'

David chuckled and turned his attention back to Caitlin. 'I'm sorry about that. You don't want to have to listen to our family goings-on. I can't tell you how great it is to see you again.' He looked her over appreciatively. 'You're absolutely gorgeous, even more so than I remember, and you were stunning back then. Are you going to be staying around here for long? That's your mother's place next door, isn't it?'

She nodded. 'I'm coming back to the village permanently. I'll be living with Mum until I can find a place of my own...for a few months, at least. That should give me time to find somewhere suitable.'

'Wow, that's fantastic.' He moved his chair closer

to hers. 'We could perhaps get together, you and I—go for a meal, have a drink, drive out to a nightclub in town. It'll be fun; what do you say—?'

'Don't even think about it, David,' Brodie cut in sharply, perhaps with more force than he'd intended. His eyes narrowed on his brother. 'I saw her first—way back when we were teenagers and now since she's come back to the village. Besides, she deserves someone with more integrity and staying power than you possess.'

'Oh yeah?' David's dark brows shot up. 'And since when were you the man to offer those things? You—the man who never settles with one woman for more than a few months at a time. I don't think so, bro. Get ready to move aside, man. Brother or no brother, this is a fair fight and Caity's a jewel worth fighting for. This is war.'

'Uh…do you two mind? Have you quite finished?' Caitlin looked from one to the other, deciding it was time to butt in before things got out of hand. 'I'll decide what happens where I'm concerned, and right now neither of you is in the running. From my point of view, you're probably both as bad as each other. So back off, both of you!'

David stared at her, looking reasonably chastened. 'Sorry, Caity.'

He soon recovered, shaking himself down and saying cheerfully, 'I think I'll go and hunt out a bottle of something from Brodie's bar, if that's okay?' He glanced enquiringly at his brother.

'That's fine.'

David left them, taking himself off into the house. Brodie looked back at Caitlin, a trace of amusement in his expression.

'You were always one to speak your mind,' he said. 'I like that about you, Caitlin. It's the barn incident all over again. You've never been prepared to put up with things you're not happy about.'

His smile was crooked as he added softly, 'Years ago, you told me we were a pair of hooligans on the rampage, David and me, not to be trusted. You weren't ever going to date either one of us…me especially, you said.' His face took on a sober expression. 'No matter how hard I tried, you'd never let me persuade you otherwise.'

'So the message was received and understood.' She smiled at him as she took a long swallow of her drink.

'Perfectly.' He returned her gaze, his blue eyes glinting. 'Of course, it's always been out there between us as something of a challenge. I know you like me and there were times when you might have been tempted to go against your better judgement. You do realise, don't you, that my feelings towards you have never changed?'

'Oh, you can't be sure about that,' she said. Even as she tried to make less of it, a tingle of excitement ran through her. 'It's been a long time… Perhaps you only want what you can't have.'

'I don't know, Caity. Perhaps you're right. Things happened when I was a teenager, things that made me question who I am and what I could expect out of life. I always wanted you, that's for sure. I just wasn't certain that I deserved you. I still have doubts, but seeing you again has brought all those feelings back to the surface.'

The breath caught in her throat but she ran her finger idly around the rim of her glass to give herself time to think. Why would he feel he didn't deserve her? Was it because of his behaviour back then, because it had been out of control?

Surely now, more than ever, she had to guard her heart against being hurt?

She said slowly, cautiously, 'It isn't going to happen, I'm afraid. I think we both know that. I'm totally off men right now. They're far too fickle for my liking.'

'Hmm.' He studied her, taking in the faint droop of her soft, pink lips. 'We'll have to see about that.'

CHAPTER THREE

'I KNOW IT'S going to be terribly difficult for you this afternoon,' Caitlin's mother said worriedly. She was sitting in a chair by her hospital bed; now she shifted uncomfortably, wincing at a twinge of pain in her hip.

'Yes.' Caitlin's answer was brief. The day of the wedding had come around all too soon for her liking. Her emotions were all churned up inside her, though it wasn't only the forthcoming nuptials that bothered her. A fortnight had gone by since her mother had first come into hospital and after a brief spell at home she had been readmitted. It was distressing.

'Your aunt's desperate for everything to go off smoothly. She's been stressed about one thing and another for some time now.' Her mother's grey-blue eyes were troubled. She winced again, moving carefully as she tried to get comfortable. Small beads of perspiration had formed on her brow. 'She keeps saying how you and Jenny used to be so close.' She frowned. 'I wish I could be there to give you some support.'

Caitlin nodded, acknowledging her anxieties. 'I know.' Soothingly, she dabbed her mother's brow with a damp cloth. There was no way she could leave hospital, let alone go to her niece's wedding.

Instead of making good progress in the last couple of weeks, a nasty infection had set in around the site of the surgical incision, causing her mother a lot of pain and discomfort. Caitlin was worried about her. The consultant had inserted tubes in the wound to try to drain away the infected matter but it was turning out to be a slow process. No one knew how the infection had started but Caitlin suspected it had crept in when the dressing was changed.

'I'm pretty sure Jenny hasn't told her family that Matt and I were already a couple when they met,' she commented softly.

Her mother's brows rose in startled disbelief. 'Oh, you don't think so? Heavens, that hadn't occurred to me. It's probably the general stress of the wedding that's getting to her.'

Of course, if Caitlin didn't turn up for the celebrations this afternoon, her aunt would soon realise something was badly amiss and would want to know what was going on, wouldn't she? Caitlin felt more despondent than ever. Even more reason why she should go along to the event—yet all her instincts were clamouring for her to stay away.

She pushed her own problems to one side and sent her mother a quick, sympathetic look. 'It's rotten for you to be stuck in hospital today of all days. I know you were looking forward to seeing Aunty Anne and having a good chat—but she did say she would come and see you as soon as she could get away.'

'Yes, I'll look forward to that.' Distracted momentarily, her mother patted the magazines that littered the bed. 'At least I have plenty of reading material to keep me occupied in the meantime. Thank you for these.' She smiled. 'So how's the new job going? It was good of Brodie to set you on, wasn't it?'

'It was...' He'd been nothing but kind and helpful so far, but Caitlin couldn't help but think he had an ulterior motive. Hadn't he more or less said so that afternoon in his garden? He wanted to change her mind about men—and about him in particular. Could he do that? A tingle of alarm ran through her at the prospect. Of course he couldn't. That would be unthinkable. Talk about jumping from the frying pan into the fire. When he'd left the village years ago, she'd tried to forget about him, put him from her mind. It had been far too upsetting to dwell on what might have been.

'It's going all right so far, I think,' she said. 'The unit runs very smoothly—everyone knows their job and we all seem to work well together. I'm sure a lot of it's down to Brodie being in charge. He's very organised and efficient, and extremely good with people. Somehow, he always manages to get them to do what he wants.' It was remarkable how people responded to his innate charm.

Her mother nodded agreement. 'I'm amazed how well he's doing. Whoever would have guessed he'd turn his life around like that? I mean, I always liked him, but when he went so completely off the rails as a teenager it was upsetting. His poor mother didn't know where to turn.'

'Hmm.' Brodie's problems had started some time before his mother's death and Caitlin had never been able to find out the root cause. 'Maybe leaving the village was the making of him. He had no choice but to fend for himself, and I suppose that was bound to make a man of him. Of course,' she added with a wry inflection, 'Discovering he had an inheritance must have been a huge boost.'

Her mother nodded. 'True, but he could have gone the other way, you know, and squandered it. Instead, he put it to good use. I think he turned out all right. He seems to be a good man, now, anyway.' She frowned. 'Though I have heard he's still restless, still can't settle.' She sighed then hesitated, sending Caitlin a quick look. 'Does he mind that you keep coming up here to see me in the middle of your work?'

Caitlin shook her head. 'No, not at all…in fact, he's encouraged me to come to see you. He wants to know how you are. He's very fond of you. Anyway, I use my break times to slip away from the unit, so there's no real problem.' She glanced at her watch and gave her mother a rueful smile. 'In fact, I should be heading back there right now. I've a couple of small patients I need to see before I can go home.'

'All right, love. You take care. I'll see you later.'

'Yes. Try to get some rest.' Caitlin gave her a hug and hurriedly left the room.

Brodie was checking X-ray films on the computer when she returned to the children's unit a few minutes later. He shot her a quick glance as she came over to the desk to pick up her patient's file. 'How is your mother?'

'She's not feeling too good at the moment, I'm afraid...though she'll never complain.' She pulled a face. 'The site of the incision's still infected and she's feverish. The doctor's prescribed a different course of antibiotics and some stronger painkillers, so all we can do now is wait and see how she goes on. This setback isn't helping with her rehabilitation.' She sighed. 'It's all been a bit of a blow. We were hoping she'd be able to come home in a couple of days' time but that's definitely not on the cards now.'

'I imagine she's upset about missing the wedding?'

'Oh yes, that too.' Her mouth made a crooked line. 'I think she's secretly hoping I'll be her eyes and ears there. I imagine she'll want to see a video of the highlights on my phone—though she won't come out and ask.'

He smiled. 'It would probably help her to feel better about not being there, but I'm sure she's more concerned about your feelings.'

'Mmm. Maybe.' Even at this late stage Caitlin was desperately looking for a way out. Perhaps she could manufacture a sudden headache that would incapacitate her? Or maybe her car would develop an imaginary mechanical fault at the last minute?

Matt and Jenny were being married mid-afternoon, so as to accommodate relatives who were travelling from some distance away, and Caitlin was becoming more and more twitchy as the morning wore on. In a way, she was glad she'd chosen to come into work for a few hours to keep her from thinking too deeply about the situation. From when she'd woken earlier today, her whole body had been in a state of nervous tension.

She skim-read the notes in her four-year-old patient's file. 'I have to go and look in on the little boy who has pneumonia,' she told Brodie. 'I sent him for an X-ray before I went to see Mum and I'm hoping the results are back by now. He's not at all well: breathing fast, high temperature… He's on antibiotics and supplemental oxygen as well as steroid medication. Hopefully, it should all start to have an effect soon.'

'You're talking about Jason Miles?' Brodie brought up the boy's details on the computer. 'Here we are. Radiology have sent the films through.'

Laying the file down on the table, she studied the images on screen and frowned. 'That looks like an air-filled cyst on his lung, doesn't it? No wonder he's uncomfortable, poor little thing.'

'It does. What do you plan to do?'

'I'll leave it alone for now—it's best to avoid surgical intervention, I think. I'll put him on intravenous cefuroxime and see if that will do the trick. As the pneumonia improves, the cyst should start to disappear.'

He nodded. 'Good. I think you're right. That's probably the best course for now.' He sent her a sideways glance. 'Is he your last patient for today?'

'I just want to look in on Sammy to see how his fractured bone is healing. He went home for a while, didn't he, with a social worker overseeing things… but he's back in today for a check-up?' She frowned. 'Do you still think the other earlier fractures are suspicious? I know the social worker pushed for police action and Sammy's parents are distraught... They're overwhelmed by all the accusations being laid at their door. They're due to appear in court soon —he could be taken into foster care. Yet they do seem to be a genuine couple to me.'

He was silent for a moment or two, thinking it through. 'You could be right about the parents. I've spoken to them about taking extra precautions with him, though they insisted they were already being really careful.' His brow creased. 'I'm beginning to wonder if we aren't dealing with some underlying disease that could cause the bones to fracture more easily than most. I think we should get a blood sample for DNA testing along with a small skin biopsy and send them off to the lab. We'll need to keep an eye on the boy in the meantime—have him seen in the clinic on a regular basis.'

'Okay. I can set that up before I leave.'

'Good.' He leaned back in his chair and studied her. 'So, I'll come and pick you up after lunch, shall I— around two-thirty? Then we'll head off to the church?'

'Um...' She ought to have been expecting it but the reminder still caught her off guard. 'I...um...well, you know, I was thinking... It might be embarrassing for Jenny to have me there. I know her mother dealt with a lot of the invitations, so I'm not necessarily Jenny's choice as a guest.'

She wriggled her shoulders slightly. 'Perhaps it would be for the best if I were to send a message to say something's cropped up—an emergency at the hospital or some such. I mean, it's true, isn't it? Jason's very poorly—maybe I should come back here to keep an eye on him?'

He shook his head, his mouth quirking a fraction. 'You know that won't work, Caitlin, don't you? You're not an emergency doctor and we have people here who will take excellent care of him. You're trying to find excuses, when instead perhaps you should be facing up to things. You need to deal with this, once and for all, instead of running away.'

Her grey eyes narrowed on him. Coming on top of all her worry and apprehension, his comment seemed a bit like a reprimand.

'Are you saying I'm a coward?' After everything she'd been through, the thought irritated her, and she reacted in self-defence. 'Why should I be the one who has to suffer? *They're* in the wrong. Why do *I* have to pay the price for what *they* did?'

'Because you won't be able to live with yourself if you don't,' he said in a matter-of-fact tone. 'Sooner or later, you have to face up to the fact that it's over between you and Matt. He's in love with someone else. See it and believe it. Isn't that what you're running away from? The truth?'

'How can you be so heartless?' Her voice broke and she stared at him, frustration welling up inside her. 'Do you have no feelings? Is that all relationships are to you—off with the old and on with the new?' A muscle flicked in his jaw but he remained silent and she went on. 'What about the aftermath? It's so easy for you to shrug things off, isn't it?'

Resentment grew in her and all her past dealings with him came bubbling up to the surface. 'No wonder Beth was so hurt when you finished things with her. You didn't care too much, though, did you? Not deep down. As far as you were concerned it was just one of those things that happened from time to time. You changed your mind about her, didn't like getting in too deep, and decided to call a halt. It didn't matter to you how she felt, did it? You were ready to move on and you weren't about to look back.' She stared at him. 'How could I ever have believed you might have changed?'

'So this is all about me, now, is it?' His dark brows lifted. 'I don't think you can get out of it that easily, Caitlin, by turning everything around. You're the one who has the problem and the best way you can deal with it is to put on a brave face and go to the wedding.' His voice softened a little. 'I'll be there with you,' he said coaxingly. 'Show Matt you've found someone else, that it doesn't matter what he's done—that you and I are a couple, if that will make you feel any better.'

She looked at him aghast. 'You think I can do that with you—pretend that we're together, that we care about each other?' She gritted the words out between her teeth. 'I don't think so, Brodie. I'm not that much of an actress.'

To her surprise, he flinched, his head going back a fraction at her sharp retort. Obviously her dart had struck home.

'Is it such an alien concept? I'm sorry you feel that way,' he said quietly. 'Finding you after all this time, I was hoping we might be able to put the past behind us and move on, get to know one another all over again. I've always had feelings for you, Caitlin, and I thought this might be a chance for us to get together.'

Still upset, she said tautly, 'Did you? That's unfortunate, because it isn't very likely to happen. We're all out of fairy godmothers right now.'

She picked up Jason's file from the table and walked away from him. For her own peace of mind, she needed to put some distance between them. Her nerves were stretched to the limit. Deep down, though, she knew she'd gone too far, knew she'd said too much.

As she drove home some time later, she warred with herself over the way she'd behaved, over what she ought to do. Through it all she was still trying to find ways out of the mess she was in. How could she get out of going to this wretched wedding?

Back at home, it was some time before she could bring herself to admit that maybe Brodie was right. She couldn't keep running forever, could she?

She fed the hens and tried to think things through as she scattered corn and dropped a couple of carrots into the rabbit's run. By now the geese had learned to accept her and were grateful for a bucket of greens and a bowl of food pellets.

Why was she so convinced she could bury her feelings by pushing them aside, by hiding them away? Matt was marrying someone else. He didn't love her any more. Perhaps he'd never truly loved her because, if he had, surely this would never have happened? What was it Brodie had said? *Was he looking to get out of the relationship?* Perhaps Matt hadn't been consciously looking but somewhere a chink had opened up in the wall and opportunity had crept in.

She went back inside the house. She had to face up to this once and for all: go along to the wedding or berate herself for her weakness for the rest of her days.

Besides, no matter how bad she felt for Caitlin's dilemma, her mother would be desperate for pictures... She rolled her eyes, looking briefly heavenward. Then she took a deep breath and went upstairs to get ready. She'd burnt her boats with Brodie but somehow, when she met up with him at the church later on, she would have to do her best to put things right.

She'd bought her dress especially for the occasion, hoping it might help to boost her confidence. It was knee-length with a ruched bodice and a cross-over draped skirt that fell in soft folds over her hips. A small scattering of spangles embellished the thin straps at the shoulders.

She pinned up her hair so that a few errant curls softened the line of her oval face then carefully applied her make-up, adding a touch of lipstick to her full mouth. A final spray of perfume and she was ready.

The doorbell rang as she came down the stairs. Her eyes widened as she opened the door to find Brodie standing on the doorstep.

He whistled softly. 'Wow!' he said in a breathless kind of way. 'You look beautiful. Are you quite sure there isn't a fairy godmother lurking around?' He peered into the hallway as if searching for the mythical figure. 'How else could you have made such a stunning transformation in such a short time?'

'Well, maybe she turns out for the odd emergency.' She smiled at him. 'You look terrific,' she murmured, giving him an appreciative glance. His grey suit was immaculate, finished off with a silk waistcoat and matching grey silk tie. 'I didn't really expect to see you here this afternoon after what I said to you earlier.'

He made a vague gesture with his shoulders. 'I guessed you were under a bit of a strain. We all say things we regret sometimes. Anyway, I was pretty sure you would change your mind about going.'

'What gave you that idea?'

'Keeping the family peace is important to you. Besides, I knew you wouldn't let your mother down, not when she's in hospital wanting to know what's going on.'

She laughed. 'You're right about that. Thanks for turning up.'

He gave her a crooked smile. 'We'll put in an appearance, then, if only to eat the canapés and drink the wine?'

'That sounds okay to me.'

'Good. The taxi's here already.'

She collected her bag and a light jacket then went with him to the waiting cab. 'Will your brother be coming to the wedding?' she asked. 'I haven't seen him around.'

He nodded. 'He's at the studios going over the screenplay for *Murder Mysteries* but he'll come straight from there.'

They arrived at the church in time to be seated by the ushers; in the hushed atmosphere, Caitlin's gremlins came back in full force. She had to steel herself against a rising tide of panic. She would not faint, she would not be sick, she wouldn't make a fool of herself by breaking out in a sweat… No way…this couldn't be happening…

Brodie reached out to her, covering her fingers with his palm. 'It's okay, you're doing fine,' he said softly. His voice and that reassuring touch of his hand on hers helped to calm her. 'Just think how many generations of families have married in this church. Weren't your parents married here?'

She nodded. 'Were yours?'

'Yes.' He looked around, frowning at something, and she saw that his brother had entered the church. The usher was showing Brodie's father and him to a seat a few rows behind theirs. She felt Brodie stiffen.

'You still haven't managed to make up with your father?' she asked in a whisper.

'No.'

'I'm sorry. I thought you might have had a chance to talk by now. Maybe you could have another go at the reception? A family occasion like this might be the ideal time for you to get together and patch things up.'

'Maybe, though I think it'll take more than a patch to mend things between us.'

The wedding service passed in a blur for Caitlin. Jenny looked beautiful in ivory silk, and Matt was tall and elegant in his tailored grey suit and silver cravat. Watching them, she felt a lump form in her throat, a sadness welling up in her for what might have been. A sick feeling burgeoned inside her.

Brodie clasped her hand firmly as they stood to sing the hymns. He wasn't about to let her sway or lose control and she would be eternally grateful to him for that.

At last the service was over and they went outside to pose for photographs. She gulped in a lungful of fresh air. Brodie's arm went around her waist and she glanced up at him briefly, reading the intent, unmistakeable message in his gaze. He would be there for her. She was safe. She gave him a faint, answering smile and, when she looked away a moment or two later, feeling calmer, she saw that Matt was watching her, a bemused, quizzical expression on his face.

Yes, it was perfectly true, she was safe…for now, at least.

They went on from the church to a hotel where a wedding banquet had been prepared for them. Everything was beautifully set out with lovely flower arrangements as centrepieces on the dressed tables and soft floor-length drapes at the windows reflecting the silver-and-lilac colour scheme.

'Have something to eat…you'll feel better for it.' Brodie wasn't listening to any excuses about not being hungry as they sat down at their allotted table. He tempted her with delicate morsels of crispy confit duck and delicious forkfuls of beetroot carpaccio flavoured with lemon, dill and finely chopped red onion. He held them teasingly to her lips until she capitulated.

'All right, all right,' she laughed. 'I'll eat.' She

glanced at all that was on offer. 'It looks wonderful,' she admitted.

David and Brodie's father were seated close by but, although the brothers spoke to one another in a relaxed fashion, the tension between Brodie and his father was noticeable. The older man was straight-backed, uncomfortable, speaking in monosyllabic tones, while Brodie for his part seemed guarded. He tried several times to open up a conversation with his father but the result was stilted and went nowhere. Caitlin watched them cautiously, slowly sipping her red wine.

Eventually, to her relief, the dinner and the speeches were over and it was time for music and dancing. Matt and Jenny started things off with the first waltz then Brodie took Caitlin's hand in his and led her on to the dance floor.

He drew her into his arms and held her close. 'I've been wanting to do this, it seems, like for ever,' he murmured. 'You're gorgeous, Caity, irresistible. And you've been so brave—I wanted to hold you tight and tell you everything was going to be fine. You're doing really well.'

She was glad of his embrace just then. It saved her from thinking about Matt and Jenny whirling around the dance floor locked in each other's arms. 'I couldn't have done any of this without you,' she said with a rueful frown. 'I think I'd still be at the hospital with Jason, if it wasn't for you.'

He made a wry smile. 'I'm sorry if I upset you back then. Matt's a fool for going off with someone else. I can't imagine why he would behave that way—you're beautiful and fun to be with and I can't think what went wrong between you to make him do that. I hate to see you hurting, Caitlin, but I wanted to shake you out of your negative state of mind. You wouldn't have felt right if you'd backed off.'

'Maybe not.' She gave in to the flow of the music and succumbed to the lure of his arms as he swept her around the dance floor. He held her easily, close but not too close, their bodies brushing tantalisingly as they moved to the rhythm of the band.

Perhaps it was the warming effect of the wine but it wasn't long before she found herself relaxing, wanting more, wanting to lean in to him and feel the safety of his arms wrapped even more securely around her.

'I think you should let me take a turn around the floor with Caity,' David said, coming over to them as the musicians took a break. He looked his brother in the eye. 'You've had her to yourself for long enough.' He glanced back at the seating area. 'Besides, it's time you had another go at talking to Dad.'

Brodie frowned, giving way reluctantly to his younger brother. 'Two minutes,' he said. 'That's all you're getting.'

'As if.' David's retort was short and to the point.

'Wow, what it is to be popular,' Caitlin said with a smile as David took her hand in his. The music changed to disco style and they moved in time to the beat opposite one another. She shot a quick look to where Brodie and his father stood side by side. 'I don't understand what went wrong between them. They were always uneasy with one another, I know that, but it was so much worse when he turned fifteen. And then, after your mother died, the animosity spiralled out of control.' She shook her head in bewilderment. 'Do you think they'll ever sort things out?'

'I suppose it's possible, now that Brodie's come back to the village to stay—at least for a while. He's never been one for putting down roots, has he? But that's probably down to the way things were back when he was a teenager. In a way, he's out of sync with the world and he can't seem to find his place in it. He can't settle but he can't move on because nothing feels right.'

She shook her head. 'None of that makes any sense to me.'

'No, well, it's up to Brodie to explain, I think. I wouldn't want to step in and cause even more chaos by trying to fathom what goes on in his mind. All I know is things won't be right with Brodie until he and Dad find some kind of closure.'

They danced for a while then David offered to go and get her a glass of wine from the bar. A late-evening buffet had been set out and there was a mouth-watering selection of food on display. Suddenly hungry, she chose a selection of West Country beef, mixed salad and warm, buttered new potatoes.

'You're feeling better, I see,' Brodie murmured, coming to stand alongside her and filling his plate with savoury tart, a charcuterie of meats, prosciutto, duck liver pâté and sausage, along with ricotta cheese.

'Yes, much better,' she said, surprised at herself. 'It's all down to wine, good food and the company, I expect.'

His gaze moved over her. 'Especially the company, I hope?'

She smiled. 'Of course.' She dipped her fork into a summer-berry meringue and revelled in the combination of sweet and tart flavours as the dessert melted on her tongue. They chatted for a while, enjoying the food, drinking wine and sharing reminiscences with David when he returned to the buffet table.

'I'm supposed to go and dance with the bridesmaids,' David said, draining his glass and placing it down on a tray. 'Jenny's orders. I think the blonde has the hots for me...except it could be simply that she's hoping to get a part in *Murder Mysteries*.' He squared his shoulders. 'Ah, well; a man has to do what a man has to do...'

They laughed and watched him go. 'Shall we go outside and get some air in the garden?' Brodie suggested when they had finished eating. 'I've been to a function here before—the terrace is lovely at this time of night. You can wander along the pathways and breathe in the night-scented flowers.'

'Okay, that sounds good.' She walked with him to the open doors that led out on to the balustraded terrace. It was, as he said, lovely, with soft, golden lighting and the fragrance of wisteria that bloomed in profusion against the wall. Further away from the building, alongside the pathways, were occasional trellises covered with honeysuckle and flowerbeds where sprawling nicotiana gave up its perfume.

As they walked, he put his arm around her and she loved the feeling of closeness. The night air was warm and full of promise. It would be all too easy to fall for Brodie, she conceded. He was attentive, supportive and he had the knack of boosting her confidence when she needed it most. But he wasn't the staying kind, was he? He'd never been one for commitment.

'How did you get on with your father?' she asked. 'I saw you talking to him. He seemed to have lightened up a bit.'

'He's had a drink or two. I guess that's the key to loosening him up and getting him to overlook my shortcomings, although he's never going to feel for me the same way he feels for David. He always favoured him.' He said it without rancour, as a statement of fact. 'When David came along the world was a brighter place and my father expected me to watch over him and keep him safe.'

She sent him a quick look. 'You didn't seem to mind doing that.'

'I didn't, not at all. We fought sometimes, we got into scrapes, but we were brothers. I think the world of him and I'd do anything for him.' His expression became sombre. 'My one regret was that I had to leave him behind when I left home. David didn't forgive me for a long time. He hated that I'd left.'

'I liked the way you took it on yourself to watch out for him. I'm sure he knew you weren't left with much of a choice but to go away, back then.'

She looked up at him as they stopped in the shade of a spreading oak tree. Moonlight filtered through its branches, casting them in a silvery glow. She leaned

back against the broad trunk of the tree and he stood
in front of her, sliding one arm around her waist.

She'd always liked him—wanted him, even—but
always there had been this wariness whenever she was
with him. Perhaps it was her youth that had held her
back from him in those far-away days, the knowledge
that he was at odds with the world, always in trouble,
yet he didn't seem to care... There had been that element of danger about him. There still was. Being with
him set her on a path of uncertainty—a path that could
surely only lead to heartbreak because she still yearned
for him. Even as she gazed up into his eyes and read
the desire glittering in their fiery depths she recognised
the folly of what she was contemplating.

'Caity,' he murmured, lifting a hand to brush her
cheek gently. 'You're so lovely. You take my breath
away.'

He bent his head towards her, his face so close to
her that his lips were just a whisper away from hers.
She longed to have him kiss her but she was confused,
her emotions a maelstrom of doubt and insecurity. This
day had started off with so many echoes of unhappy
feelings, she didn't know how she could have come so
far to wanting this...

A soft sound drifted on the night air, a footfall on
the path just a short distance away, and as she looked
out into the shadows she became aware of Jenny and
Matt walking along the path, talking quietly to one another. They paused and stopped to gaze up at the moon.

Caitlin closed her eyes to shut out the image and
then looked back at Brodie. His gaze was dark with

yearning, smoky with desire; in that instant she lost herself, caught up in the flow of that heated current. She needed his strength right then, his powerful arms around her, everything that meant shelter and protection from the outside world. She ran her fingers up over his chest, lacing them around the strong column of his neck.

His kiss was gentle, coaxing, a slow, glorious exploration of everything she had to offer. His lips brushed hers, the tip of his tongue lightly, briefly, tracing the full curve of her mouth, seeking her response. She kissed him in return and in a feverish surge of passion he drew her close, easing her into the welcoming warmth of his taut, muscular thighs.

Her soft curves meshed with his hard, masculine frame and a ragged sigh escaped her, breaking in her throat. He kissed her thoroughly, desperately, his hands moving over her in an awed, almost reverent journey of discovery.

'Brodie...' She didn't know what she wanted to say...just his name was enough. She wanted him, needed him, longed for him to make her his.

And yet...wasn't he too strong, too male, too much of a driving force that would sweep her up and carry her along with him until he had done with her and was ready to move on? Perhaps she had always cared too much... She'd cared for Matt and he'd walked all over her; she cared for Brodie and he would eventually push her away. Could she handle that rejection, that awful nothingness that was bound to come?

But, then again, why shouldn't she experience once

and for all the joy that was his to give, theirs to share, a memory to cherish for all time? She needed him, craved his touch. Somehow in these last few heated moments she had lost all sense of caution, thrown inhibition to waft on the night breeze.

'Caitlin?' He spoke softly, urgently. 'I want you; you know that, don't you?'

She nodded, her gaze fixed on him, intent. 'Yes. I want you too.' It was a whisper.

A soft gasp escaped him. 'I don't want you to regret anything that happens between us… Do you understand what I'm saying?'

'Of course.' Her eyes widened, becoming luminous with unshed tears. 'Of course I understand. But why are you saying this?' Why was he bringing it out into the open, making her think about what she wanted to keep back?

'I know you only kissed me because Matt was there on the path with Jenny,' he said. 'I know why you did it and that's all right. I'm okay with that. I can handle it—at least, I think I can.'

He cupped her face lightly in his hands. 'And I know that you want me too, if only for the moment. But I need you to be sure about what you're doing. I have feelings too, you know. You mean too much to me, and I don't want to ruin what we have by sweeping you off your feet and then having you regret it.'

'I didn't set out to do this.' Her hands were trembling as she drew them back down his chest. 'I didn't mean for it to happen. I'm sorry,' she whispered brokenly. Tears trickled down her cheeks. 'Have...have they gone?'

He nodded. 'They've gone.'

'I'm sorry,' she said again. 'I don't know what I was thinking. I'm so sorry, Brodie.'

'Maybe there's a chance you could change your mind?' His dark eyes were brooding.

'No, there isn't.' She looked up at him, her whole body shaking. 'I can't do this.'

He pulled in a deep breath and seemed to steel himself. 'It's okay. Come on, then. I'll take you home.'

CHAPTER FOUR

THE KNOCK AT the door came as Caitlin was getting on with some chores upstairs before getting ready for work on Monday morning. She wasn't due to start her shift until later that day so up till now she'd been taking things at a fairly relaxed pace. Now, though, as the knocking came again, she frowned. It couldn't be Brodie wanting to see her, could it?

She wasn't ready to face him yet. She was still in shock from the way things had turned out on Saturday evening at the wedding reception. How could she have let things get out of hand that way? But wasn't she secretly, deep down, wishing she'd made a different decision? Why couldn't she have let things take their course, see where they led? The longing haunted her.

She hurried downstairs to answer the door. She would have to see him and try to work with him once more as if nothing had happened. How was she going to do that?

It would be so difficult…though how much worse would it have been if she'd given in to her feelings for him? Would she have regretted it the next morning?

Maybe not. A wave of heat surged through her. The more she thought about it, the more she had to admit that she really had wanted him for himself and not just because Matt had been there to muddle her thinking. Brodie had been wrong when he'd thought that; in truth it was Brodie who had managed to turn her world upside down, not Matt.

And how could that be? Matt was the one she was supposed to care for. He'd been the love of her life, hadn't he? Or had he? The truth was beginning to dawn on her and it was much harder to handle than she might have expected.

Could it be that Matt had been the consolation prize, the runner-up, the one she'd turned to because wanting Brodie all those years ago had been an impossible dream? She groaned softly in frustration. Why did Brodie have to come back into her life and confuse her this way?

The knocking came again, getting louder, and she called out, 'Okay, I'm coming.'

She opened the door, half-expecting to see Brodie standing in the porch, but instead she looked down to see a young girl of around ten years old. She recognised her from the village.

'Hello, Rosie. What can I do for you? Is everything all right?' Rosie didn't look all right. She was breathing fast, as though she'd been running, and her expression was anxious.

'Oh!' Rosie seemed put out. 'I thought you'd be Mrs Braemar.' The girl shook her head at her mistake. 'Hi. It's just—she always looks after the animals.' Rosie frowned and tried to gather her thoughts. 'We found a dog, see, a girl dog—along the lane—my friend and me. She stayed with it, Mandy did. We were playing in the fields, looking for wild flowers on our way to school—there are some summer activities going on there. I think the dog might be hurt.' She pulled a face. 'She doesn't want to move. Will you come and look at her?'

Caitlin thought quickly. The best place for an injured dog would be at the vet's surgery but that was way across town and she had to be at work this morning. Even so, if the animal was injured...

'Give me a minute, Rosie. I'd better call on the doctor next door and see if we can borrow his pick-up truck to go and fetch her.' Old Mr Martin had left the truck behind when he'd sold the house to Brodie and from what she'd heard it was still in working order. Brodie had used it to take unwanted bits and pieces of furniture from the house when he'd moved in.

'Okay.' Rosie prepared to wait patiently.

Caitlin rang Brodie's doorbell, more than a little apprehensive about meeting up with him once more. She'd not seen sight nor heard sound of him since the early hours of Sunday morning when the taxi cab had dropped them both off at home. It had been a moment fraught with tension and Brodie had acknowledged that, reaching for her, wanting to hold her once more. To her everlasting regret, she'd made an excuse and turned from him in a panic.

Now, though, he wasn't answering his door, so she

pressed the bell again more firmly until eventually she heard him padding down the stairs.

'Hi there.' Brodie was frowning as he opened the door, concentrating on rubbing at his damp hair with a towel. 'What's the problem?' Caitlin guessed he'd hastily pulled on trousers and a shirt after his shower. His black hair glistened and his skin was faintly damp where his shirt was open at the neck. He looked... He was breathtaking... She swallowed hard.

'Um...I...I wondered if...'

'Oh...hi, Caitlin.' He blinked, collecting himself, as if seeing her clearly for the first time. He straightened, suddenly alert, heat glimmering in his blue eyes. 'Come in.' He stood back to allow her access but frowned when she hesitated. 'Is something wrong? Is it your mother?'

'No...no, it's not Mum.' Though that was a worry in itself. She'd spent some time with her mother at the hospital yesterday and she'd not seemed well at all.

He looked beyond her, saw Rosie and frowned again. 'Has something happened?'

'Rosie's found a dog. She thinks it's hurt; I wondered if I could borrow the pick-up truck to go and get it. I don't know how badly it's injured.'

'Sure. Uh—give me a minute and I'll come with you. You may need a hand to lift it.' Brodie went along the hallway to dispose of the towel and grab his keys from a hook in the kitchen. Almost as an afterthought, he said, 'I'll get a blanket,' and took the stairs two at a time. A moment later he was back, saying, 'Okay, let's go, shall we?'

He smiled at Rosie and helped her into the cab of the truck, waiting while Caitlin climbed into the cab alongside the girl. 'Away we go, then. Show us where you found the dog, Rosie.'

'It's along the lane, near a lay-by,' Rosie said. 'We were playing by the stile. I don't think the dog belongs to anyone in the village—at least, I've never seen it before.'

They drove the short distance to the lay-by then they all piled out of the truck to go and see where the dog lay on its side in a wild-flower meadow by the stile. Rosie's friend was sitting down beside the animal, a golden-haired terrier, gently stroking its head.

'Hi, Mandy,' Caitlin said, going to sit beside her on the dew-misted grass. 'How's she doing?'

Mandy shook her head. 'She hasn't moved.'

'Poor thing, she looks exhausted.' Caitlin checked the dog over. 'Heavens, she's pregnant. Quite heavily pregnant, I'd say.'

Brodie knelt down beside them, lightly running his hand along the terrier's flank. 'She's very cold,' he said. He carefully examined the skin at the back of her neck, adding, 'And from the way her skin reacts she's dehydrated as well.'

Caitlin frowned. 'There's no name tag or anything to identify her. I wonder if she was abandoned in the lay-by last night? She must have wandered around for a while before settling down here.'

'More than likely. Of course, she may be micro-chipped—the vet will be able to tell us that. We'll get her home and warm her up—see if she'll take a drink—

and then decide what to do from there. I can't see any
injuries anywhere but she'll need to see the vet as soon
as possible.'

He lifted the dog on to the back of the pick-up truck
and Caitlin clambered up beside her, wrapping her
in the blanket and doing her best to soothe the panting, distressed dog. 'Good girl,' she murmured softly.
'You're doing okay. We'll look after you.'

Rosie and Mandy were standing by, watching everything and looking worried. 'Will she be all right?'
Mandy asked.

'I think so,' Brodie answered. 'She's cold and worn
out—very stressed, I imagine—but we'll take good
care of her.'

'Thanks for letting us know about her,' Caitlin said
with a smile, preparing to jump down from the back of
the truck. Brodie held out a hand to her, helping her to
the ground, and for a lightning moment as their bodies
meshed a spark of stunning awareness flashed between
them. Caitlin caught her breath and tried not to show
that she'd been affected by his touch... Not easy, when
she was tingling from head to foot. Did Brodie feel the
same way? His smoke-blue gaze lingered for an instant
longer on the pink flush of her cheeks before he reluctantly let go of her hand and turned back to the girls.

'Perhaps you should get yourselves off to school
now,' he suggested quietly. 'You did well, both of you.'

'Okay. Can we come and see her later on?' Rosie's
glance went to the back of the truck.

'Of course. Any time—though she might have to
stay at the vet's surgery for a while.' Caitlin smiled.

'You saved her—you're bound to want to know how she's doing.'

The girls went on their way at last, chatting animatedly, and Caitlin climbed into the cab beside Brodie. 'I ought to stay with her until she shows signs of getting better,' she said. 'I don't know if she could cope with the journey to the vet right now. Will you be able to get someone to cover for me at the hospital if I'm a bit late?'

'Yes, don't worry about it. We need to be sure she's all right.'

'I can't imagine how anyone could abandon a dog like that. It's bad enough if it's a strong and healthy animal but a pregnant bitch… It's unbelievably cruel.'

'Yeah.' He was silent for a moment or two, deep in thought as he drove back along the lane towards the house. Caitlin noticed he drove slowly, carefully, so as to make a smooth journey for the ailing dog.

'You've always loved animals, haven't you?' she said now, thinking back to when he was a teenager. 'I remember once you found a rabbit that had been caught up in a snare and you nursed it back to health. You kept it in an outbuilding, didn't you, until it was time to set it free?'

'That's right.' He gave a wry smile as he pulled the truck into the driveway of his house and cut off the engine. 'It never did want to leave. I ended up taking it with me to medical school.'

She laughed. 'You're making it up.'

He gave her an exaggeratedly earnest look. 'Am not.

He listened to so many of my tutorials on the computer he could have taken the exam for me.'

They both chuckled then she said thoughtfully, 'There were other animals too: a stray kitten...and you kept pigeons in a shed at one time, didn't you?'

He nodded briefly. 'Until my father made me send them away. It was after my mother died. I don't think he would have done it before then because she always encouraged me in whatever I wanted to do. He said they were too messy, too noisy and there were too many of them.' He pulled a face as he sprang down from the cab. 'I suppose that last was true, in the end. More and more birds wanted to join the flock.'

'You must have found some comfort in looking after animals,' she said musingly. 'Perhaps it was because, when everything else was going wrong in your life, you always had them to turn to.'

He gave her a quick, half-amused look from under his lashes. 'You noticed that, huh?'

She nodded, being serious. 'Well, you used to come to my mother for advice on how to care for them. I could see how different you were around them. You were gentle, relaxed... Not the angry, hot-headed young man that everyone else saw.'

He smiled. 'Pets can be very calming. I was thinking of introducing pet therapy on the long-stay children's ward. It could do wonders for morale—if we bring in the right kind of animal, of course. They would have to be vetted for temperament.'

'Wow!' She stared at him. 'You amaze me, sometimes. I'd never have thought of it. But you could be right…'

He unclamped the back of the pick-up. 'We'll have to think of a name for this one. We can't keep calling her Dog or Girl, can we?'

She gave it some thought. 'How about Daisy, since we found her in a field full of them?'

He moved his head slightly, mulling it over. 'Okay,' he said at last then lifted the lethargic dog into his arms. 'Where shall I put her?'

'There's a kennel round the back…a proper one, with purpose-made quarters. I'll show you.'

She led the way to the kennel and he carefully laid Daisy down in a rigid plastic bed with half the blanket tucked under her for warmth. She didn't stir, but her brown eyes followed him and then flicked to Caitlin. 'You're safe now, Daisy,' she told her.

'I'll get another blanket,' Brodie said. 'Maybe she'll take some water.'

Caitlin stayed with her while he went to get what he needed. 'You'll be all right,' she murmured sooth-ingly, stroking the dog. 'Good girl. I'm sorry you're in this state, but you'll be fine. Good girl.'

Brodie returned with the second blanket and gen-tly laid it over the dog, tucking it in around her. She wouldn't take any water from the bowl he brought, and all they could do was stay with her and wait for her to warm up. Eventually, she accepted sips of water from Caitlin's hand.

After a while, Brodie glanced at his watch. 'I have to get to the hospital,' he said. 'I'm sorry to leave you, but at least she's a bit more responsive than she was half an hour ago. She's starting to look around a bit. Maybe she'll be strong enough for the journey to the vet now.'

'Yes. I'll take her. I'll give the vet a ring and warn him that I'm on my way.'

Brodie stood up and handed her the keys to the pick-up. 'She might as well stay in the bed. I'll carry it out to the truck.'

He made sure that Daisy was settled in the back of the pick-up once more and then glanced at his watch. 'I must go. I'll see you later. Good luck.'

'Thanks.'

She drove carefully into town, unused to the truck, and very conscious of the ailing dog in the back. It wasn't just one dog she had to worry about: the welfare of the unborn puppies was paramount too. Who could tell when Daisy had last eaten, and surely her blood pressure must be way down?

'Ah, we'll keep her warm and get her on a drip right away to replace the lost fluids and electrolytes,' the vet said, examining Daisy a short time later and giving Caitlin a friendly smile. 'She's young—around a year old, I'd say—so that's in her favour. There's no microchip, unfortunately, so we don't know who she belongs to. Anyway, leave her with us for a few hours and we'll see if we can get her to eat something. The pups seem to be okay—I can hear their heartbeats. I'd say she has a few days before she's due to give birth. I'll give you a call later to let you know how she's doing.'

'Thanks. It's such a relief to know that she's in safe

hands.' Caitlin stroked Daisy once more and said softly,
'I'll come back for you later. You'll be okay, I promise.'

She went from the vet's surgery straight to the hospital, keen to get started on her day's work. Luckily,
she wasn't late, so she wouldn't feel guilty later at taking a break to go and look in on her mother.

'We've admitted an infant, three months old,' the
staff nurse told her when she went over to the desk.
'He's feverish, with a swollen jaw and bouts of irrita-
bility and crying. I've spoken to the mother, and she's
obviously distressed, so I'm going to get her a cuppa,
calm her down and talk to her in the privacy of the
waiting room.'

'That's great, thanks, Cathy. I'll go and take a look
at him now.' It wasn't surprising that the mother was
upset. Babies couldn't tell you what was wrong with
them and it was heart-breaking to see such tiny little
things miserable and in pain.

Caitlin held the baby in her arms and rocked him
gently, trying to comfort him, and gradually he seemed
to settle. 'I'll give him a quick examination—listen to
his chest, check his ears and so on,' she told the nurse
who was assisting her. 'But I'm going to need to do
blood tests and get an X-ray to make a proper diagnosis.'

She worked as quickly and efficiently as she could,
holding the child once more when she had finished,
soothing him. 'I'll send these samples off to the lab,'
she said. 'We should get the results back fairly soon.'

After that, she looked in on all her small patients,
checking their progress and making sure they were

comfortable and cheerful. Youngsters were resilient, she found, and recovery could come about sooner than expected. Four-year-old Jason, suffering from pneumonia, was sitting up in bed watching a DVD. She smiled, pleased he'd found the strength to take an interest.

'You should go and take a break,' Brodie said, coming over to her at the desk mid-afternoon. 'You haven't stopped since you got here.'

'I wanted to make sure I pulled everything in,' she told him. 'Working part-time gives me room to manoeuvre, but I worry about fitting it all in. The wards are at full capacity right now. We're very busy.'

'You're not on your own here,' he said. 'Don't try so hard. You're doing great.'

'I hope so.'

He nodded. 'Is there any news from the vet?'

She nodded. 'He rang to say I can pick Daisy up on my way home. She's a lot better in herself now—still a bit lethargic, but at least she's taking a little food and responding to people.'

He smiled. 'That's good. I'll look in on her later, back home, if that's okay with you?'

'Of course it is.' She glanced at him, a little anxious, uncertain how they would go on together. He'd made no mention of what had happened between them at the weekend but that kiss was seared on her memory for ever... The feel of his hands on her body was imprinted on her consciousness for all time.

He placed a file in a tray on the desk and she looked at those hands—strong, capable, yet at the same time gentle, seeking, magical...

'I…um…I'll grab a sandwich and go and find out how Mum's doing,' she said hurriedly, needing to distract herself. 'She seemed to have some kind of lung problem coming on this morning, so I'm hoping they've managed to sort it out.'

'Uh-huh.' His glance moved over her, slowly, considering, but she couldn't tell what he was thinking. Had he been able to read her thoughts? Surely not? Her cheeks flushed with heat. She was in enough of a quandary already, with her emotions all over the place.

Then he said softly, 'Maybe we'll find some time to talk things over…sort things out between us…? I care about you, Caity—I always have done—more than I can say.' He pulled in a sharp breath. 'Things were super-charged for you on Saturday—I knew that—and I should have taken heed. I shouldn't have let things get out of hand. It was my fault. But maybe we can move on from there?'

'Maybe.' The word came out as a whisper, but immediately she was filled with self-doubt. What was she doing even contemplating getting together with him? 'I don't know… I don't know what I was thinking…' She'd been hurt before—she wasn't about to put herself through that heartache all over again, was she? In the cold light of day it seemed like sheer folly to go from a broken relationship straight into Brodie's arms. What was she, some kind of masochist? 'I should go…'

She hurried along to her mother's ward and sat with her for a while, calming herself down, slowing the churning in her stomach by eating one of the sandwiches from the pack she'd bought.

'You seem stressed,' her mother said, watching her from her bedside chair. 'Is…everything all…right?' She reached for a paper hanky. She sounded as though she was out of breath and Caitlin's head went back a little in alarm.

'I'm fine.' She frowned. 'Mum, what is it? Are you…?' She stood up quickly as her mother began to cough and small flecks of blood appeared on the tissue.

Swiftly, Caitlin drew the curtains around the bed and called for a nurse. 'My mother's not well,' she told her as soon as she hurried forward. She quickly explained what had happened. 'I'm concerned this is a new development. Will you ask the consultant to look in on her, please? I understand he's still here in the department.'

The girl nodded. 'He ordered scans—they were done earlier this afternoon. I'll page him right away. He's on the next ward, doing a round of his patients.'

'Thanks.' Caitlin turned back to her mother, doing her best to make her comfortable. 'It could be a chest infection,' she told her, though she thought that un-likely with all the antibiotics she'd been given for her hip problem. A stronger possibility was that a blood clot had formed in her thigh because of her mother's enforced lack of regular activity. That clot could have broken up and spread to her lungs, where an embolus would cause a blockage. That could be very bad news, depending on how large it was.

The consultant appeared at her mother's bedside within a few minutes. 'I was going to look in on you very shortly, Mrs Braemar,' he said, 'but it looks like things are taking a bit of a turn. We'll get you started on some supplemental oxygen right away.' He indicated to the nurse to set that up then continued, 'I've had a look at your scans and I'm afraid there are a few small blood clots in your lungs. That's what's causing the pain in your chest and it's why you're having difficulty breathing.'

'Is it bad?' Her mother took short, gasping breaths, clearly worried.

'Not at the moment, my dear—not as bad as it might have been. The clots are small, you see, so we can start you on medication rather than having to do any more surgery.'

'Tablets, you mean?'

'Well, we'll give you intravenous heparin to start with, because that acts quickly. It will stop the clots from getting any bigger and will prevent any more from forming. At the same time I want to start you on warfarin tablets. They take two or three days to work and once they've kicked in we can stop the heparin.'

'So the clots won't get any...bigger but they'll... stay in my lungs?' Her mother looked bewildered and Caitlin hurried to explain.

'Your body will dissolve the clots gradually,' she said. 'You should start to feel better soon.'

The consultant patted her mother's hand. 'At least your hip infection is clearing up,' he said with a reassuring smile. 'That's one blessing.'

'True.' She made a weak smile. 'Bring on the rest.'

Caitlin stayed with her while the medication was started but left a little later when she saw her mother needed to sleep. The consultant had put a light slant on things but it was one more thing that Caitlin would worry about. Her mother had always been so active and healthy prior to these setbacks. It was upsetting to see her like this.

She was subdued as she went back to the children's unit. Her mother would be all right, she told herself; the clots weren't huge and although she was uncomfortable she was in no immediate life-threatening danger.

Brodie was tending a small patient with feeding difficulties when she went to check up on the lab results for the baby she'd seen earlier. He was in a nearby bay, setting up a drip feed so that the infant would receive nourishment after an abdominal operation. The baby cooed gently, enjoying the attention as Brodie made funny faces and wiggled his fingers.

Caitlin watched them for a moment or two, her heart full. He was a natural with children. Why, oh why, did he make her care for him so much?

He, in turn, glanced at her; he must have sensed that something was wrong because his expression was quizzical.

'Something wrong with your mother?' he asked.

She nodded, not wanting to talk about it right now. She needed to keep a firm grip of herself so that she could do her job properly. Instead of saying anything more, she turned away and went to look through the lab reports.

'How is your little fellow doing?' Brodie asked later on as she went to check on the baby she'd seen earlier. He looked down at the crying infant in the cot and held out a hand to him. The baby grabbed one of his fingers and pulled, wriggling his legs. Brodie smiled.

'He's not too happy right now,' she answered. 'He's been on indomethacin to alleviate the pain and try to reduce the swelling in his jaw but I think I'll add a corticosteroid to get things working a bit better.'

'Sounds good. Have you had the test results back yet?'

She nodded. 'They showed an elevated erythrocyte sedimentation rate and raised alkaline phosphatase among other things. After seeing the X-ray films, I think we're dealing with Caffey's disease.' She grimaced faintly. 'There are changes in the bones of his jaw and his thigh bones are wider than you would expect.'

'That was well spotted, Caitlin.' He looked at her with renewed respect. 'From what I know of it, it's a rare, not very well-understood disease—with a genetic basis, I believe?'

She nodded. 'It may be passed down through a parent, or it could be through a gene mutation. Of course, it may be rare simply because a lot of cases go undiagnosed in infancy.'

'Yes—they tend to resolve themselves in early childhood.'

'True. At least I can tell his parents that the disease is generally self-limiting and the bones should remodel themselves in a few months.'

She organised the new drug regime and then checked her watch. Her shift was coming to an end and she needed to go and collect Daisy and get her settled at home. She would need to buy tins of dog meat, kibble and maybe supplements to sustain the pregnant dog—hopefully the vet would be able to advise her on what to get. A comfy, padded base for the dog bed would come in handy too.

'You're off home?' Brodie walked with her to the exit doors.

'Yes, in a few minutes. I have to drop these lab forms off in pathology first. I thought I would take a shortcut through the quadrangle.'

He walked with her, stopping by the bench seat in the dappled shade of a silver birch. 'I'm due a break,' he said. 'Do you have time to sit for a minute and tell me what's going on with your mother? I've been to see her, but she always says she's fine, and I know she isn't.'

'Oh…of course, I'm sorry. You must be worried about her too. I keep forgetting how close you were back when…' Her voice trailed away. He wouldn't want to keep being reminded of the time when his life had taken a nosedive. 'She has some pulmonary emboli that are causing her problems—they're not too large, and the consultant's starting her on anti-coagulation therapy, so that should help things to get better.' They sat down beside one another on the bench.

'I'm sorry, Caity.' He wrapped an arm around her shoulders. 'I could see you were upset when you came back down to the unit. If there's anything I can do to help you, tell me—it must be a shock, everything that's happening.'

She nodded wearily. 'Things seem to be going from bad to worse. I thought I'd have her at home by now,

Brodie.' She gazed up at him in despair. 'She was always so active, into everything; it feels so strange, seeing her the way she is now.'

'Her consultant's a good man. I'm sure he'll soon have her on the mend.' He ran his palm down her back in a comforting gesture. 'She'll be back home with you before too long, you'll see. She's a fighter, your mum. Things will soon be back to how they were.' He smiled. 'You were always such a loving family unit—you, your mum and your dad.'

'Yes, we were.'

He sighed. 'I'm almost ashamed to say I envied you back then—you seemed to have everything I was missing out on.'

She looked at him in surprise. 'I'm sorry.'

'There was always something not quite right between me and my dad.' He shrugged. 'I think your mother recognised that and that's why she took me under her wing—David too, of course, after Mum died, though somehow he seemed to cope a bit better than I did. Yet your mother must have gone through agonies when your dad passed away.'

'Yes, it was bad. It was very sudden, a heart attack that took him before we could realise what was happening. But she managed to hold things together. I think she felt she had to, for my sake...and yours. David's too.' She glanced at him. 'My father's death helped bring you and I closer together, didn't it? It gave us a stronger bond...and my mother sensed that. I think she was pleased that we talked a lot because she knew we could be good for each other. She knew you were deeply troubled—not just about your mother—and she wanted to help.'

'We needed all the support we could get. She's a lovely woman. She was like a mother to me after my mum passed away. I always felt I could talk to her. She listened—she didn't always offer advice, but she was there for me whenever I was wound up, wanting to hit out, needing to offload because of some new quarrel with my dad. She usually managed to calm me down somehow.'

Caitlin frowned. 'What did you argue about, you and your dad? I never understood it. You were the oldest child, the firstborn—I'd have expected things to be very different. But, like you said, you and your father never seemed to get on.'

His mouth flattened. 'No, we didn't. I was never sure why, but nothing I did was ever good enough for him. The one, constant feeling he showed towards me was...irritation. In the end I learned to be guarded around him, I suppose. I tried to toe the line...until, one day, we had a terrible argument and everything came to a head and boiled over. I'd had enough at that point and I decided I wasn't going to put up with his hassle any more.'

She studied him, her grey eyes troubled. 'What happened? I wish I could help, Brodie. You never spoke about it, so it must have been something major. Can you talk to me about it? Whatever it is, I promise, I'll keep it to myself.'

'I know.' He idly caressed her shoulder, drawing her to him. He moved his head so that his temple brushed her cheek and the breath caught in her lungs. She wanted to hold him to her. He said quietly, 'I trust you, where I wouldn't trust anyone else—except my brother.'

She loved the closeness, the warmth, that came from him but after a moment or two he straightened and she felt the loss acutely. Pulling herself together, remembering their surroundings, she said cautiously, 'What was the argument about?'

He gave a wry smile. 'Actually, it was about David… or, at least, me looking after him. Dad was at work on the Saturday morning—Mum had a bad headache and was lying down. I was supposed to take David to a football training session but it was damp and drizzly and on the way there he said he didn't want to go. He was never that much into football. He said he was going to hang out with a girl instead, someone we met up with along the way. He said he didn't want me tagging along—he was barely twelve and they were just pals from school, nothing more. She wanted to listen to music back at her house, so I said it was okay.'

'But it didn't work out like that?'

He shook his head. 'A bit later on they apparently decided to go for a walk by the brook. Like I said, it had been raining earlier. David was a bit overambitious— showing off, I expect—and managed to slide down a steep slope, straight into the water. It wasn't deep but he fell in and finished up soaked through and muddy. Dad caught him before he had time to change his clothes. After that it was all hell let loose. I was the one in trouble because I hadn't been with him to watch out for him.'

Caitlin was puzzled. 'But that's the kind of thing most youngsters get up to. Why would it cause such a big problem, one that lasted for years to come? Did you both overreact?'

'We certainly did—big time. Dad said I was totally irresponsible...couldn't be trusted to keep my brother out of trouble. Of course I became defensive and argued back, asked why was it all down to me...why was he putting his job on to me? He was the father, wasn't he? Not that he'd ever been a decent father to me like he had to David, the favoured one... Et cetera, et cetera; I expect you know how it goes.'

'So you went too far?'

'Oh, yes...and he lost it completely. Said I wasn't his son so why would he care about me? He didn't give two hoots about me, just put up with me for my mother's sake.'

Caitlin gasped. 'Oh, Brodie... I'm so sorry. Was it true, what he said, or had he made it up on the spur of the moment?'

Brodie moved his arm from around her and brought his hands together in his lap, clasping his fingers together. It was as though he was totally alone in that moment; she wanted to reach out, wrap her arms around him and comfort him. He was rigid, though, his whole manner isolating himself from everyone and everything.

'Oh, yes. It was true. I asked my mother and she eventually admitted it to me. She was pregnant with me when she married my father, she said. He knew… He didn't like it, because she was having someone else's child, but he married her all the same. He just never wanted me and when I came along he couldn't bring himself to make a bond.'

Caitlin reached out and laid her hand over his. 'Did your mother tell you who your real father was?'

He shook his head. 'She didn't want to talk about him; said it was a fleeting thing—she made a mistake with a man who was never going to stay around for long. He was ambitious, wanted to go back to the city where he lived, wanted to make something of himself. She was a home bird, a country girl, and she didn't think she would ever be part of his world.'

'No wonder you went off the rails. You must have been so bewildered.'

'I was angry… Not with my mother—I could understand how she might have fallen for someone and how she turned to my dad when this man went away. She was always loving towards me, and there were endless rows between her and Dad over the way he treated me. He loved her, I'm sure, but he couldn't get beyond the other man who had figured in her life and things were never easy between them. We weren't what you'd call a contented family.'

She ran her hands lightly over his forearms. 'I wish I'd known at the time. Perhaps I could have helped, instead of being mad at you for the way you behaved. I knew there was a reason but I couldn't fathom it and I didn't know how to reach you…the real you.'

He gave a crooked smile. 'That's because he went

missing for a while.' His expression was sombre. 'Perhaps part of him is still beyond reach.'

She shook her head. 'You don't mean that.'

He looked at her, taking in the vulnerable curve of her cheek and the soft fullness of her pink lips. 'I don't know—I'm still unsure about a lot of things—but it makes me feel good to know that you wanted to reach out to me.'

'I'm glad about that.' She wanted to say more—to go on talking with him, get him to open up to her—but someone stepped out into the quadrangle and they moved apart. 'I should go,' she said and he nodded.

'Me too.'

CHAPTER FIVE

'YOU'VE BEEN BUSY.' Caitlin's mother looked at the basket of fruit Caitlin had brought for her. 'That's not all come from home, has it?'

'It has, actually.' Caitlin was proud of the amount of fruit she'd managed to harvest. It was mostly being sold at the local market but she'd gathered together an assortment for the gift basket. There were early fruiting James Grieve apples, a few pears, pink-skinned Victoria plums and some of the later varieties of strawberries. 'I thought it might help to cheer you up.'

It had also given her something to do, had helped keep her occupied outside of work. It gave her less time to dwell on situations that were fast running out of her control. Brodie had given her a lot to think about with his revelations about his father. His background meant that he probably still had a lot of self-doubt and she wondered if he would ever be able to make a proper commitment to her. She was falling for him all over again but for her own self-preservation she knew she should guard against losing her heart to him.

'Bless you, it's wonderful; a real treat.' Her mother

smiled. 'Oh, it makes me long to be back home. I can't wait to get back there and see how everything's going on.'

'I'm sure it won't be too long now,' Caitlin agreed, trying to give her some encouragement. 'You're certainly looking a bit brighter. There's colour in your cheeks and you seem to be breathing a little easier.'

'I am. I'm managing to get a bit further with the walking frame now before the lack of breath stops me.'

'That's good to know.' Caitlin smiled. 'And there's a bit of news I thought you'd want to know about—David has asked if the film unit can use the smallholding as one of their sets for an episode of *Murder Mysteries*. He said they would pay well, so I said I'd ask you. I didn't really think you'd have any objection. They promise they won't leave a mess, and the filming will all be done over two or three days. I think they especially want to use the barn and the area around the hen hut.'

'Oh, how exciting! Yes, of course that's okay. It'll be so interesting to see our home on the television, won't it? I wonder what they'll make of it? Oh, I can't wait!'

Caitlin chuckled. 'I thought you'd be all right with it. David's asked if we'll be extras and take part in the filming—Brodie and me—along with some of the villagers. Brodie's a bit wary but apparently the villagers are all really keen to get in on the act.'

'I'll bet they are...' Her mother started to cough, overcome with anticipation, and Caitlin frowned. She was looking better and it was all too easy to forget how ill her mother had been.

'Don't try to talk,' she said now. 'Just rest. I'll fill you in on what's been going on.'

'Yes…' Interested to know what was going on, her mother ignored her suggestion not to speak. 'Tell me about the dog you found. How is she?'

'She's doing fine. Rosie's mother drops by whenever she can while I'm at work to make sure she's okay. She and Rosie are helping to take her for walks.'

'Isn't she about due to give birth?'

Caitlin nodded. 'Could be today, according to the vet, so Rosie said she'd keep a special eye on her. I'm not sure what to look for, except the vet said something about temperature changes—she'll get a rise in temperature and then it will drop when she's about to go into labour.'

'You'll know when she's ready.' Her mother paused, getting her breath. 'She'll probably be restless.'

'I'll look out for that. I hope she's okay.' She glanced at her mother, making sure she was all right. 'She's such a sweet-natured dog. Here, I took a picture of her on my phone…' She showed her the photo of the shaggy, golden-haired terrier and told her how the vet had said to feed her on puppy food because it was higher in nutrients and therefore good for her while she was pregnant.

'Brodie comes over every day to see her and she follows him everywhere. At least, I think it's Daisy he comes to see.' She couldn't be altogether sure. They'd taken to sharing the occasional snack supper together of an evening, alternating between the two houses. He'd not pushed anything when it came to starting any kind of relationship with her but she had the feeling he was finding it hard to stay away. She was glad about that. She liked having him around.

A wave of heat ran through her at the direction her thoughts were taking and she quickly forced her mind back to the dog.

'She's fixated on him ever since he tucked the blanket around her and offered her a pull toy and a biscuit. I think she would up sticks and go and live with him if she could.' She made a mock-peeved expression. 'I'm not certain how I feel about that—I think I'm quite put out about it.'

Her mother laughed. 'He always did have a way with the girls.'

'True.' Caitlin didn't want to go too deeply into that. Despite her misgivings she'd come closer to him in these last few days than ever before and it invoked all sorts of exhilarating and tummy-tingling sensations inside her that she'd never experienced before—not even with Matt. But falling for Brodie was definitely not on the cards, was it?

'Are you and he getting on all right?' her mother asked.

'Yes, fine.' She sent her a guarded look. 'Why wouldn't we?'

Her mother shrugged lightly. 'I know how he used to look at you and how you kept putting up barriers— you didn't want to get involved with someone who kicked against the establishment and who seemed happy to play the field. I doubt he's changed that much. He doesn't go with the crowd or let the grass grow under his feet. He has his own ideas and likes to follow through.'

She paused, pulling air into her lungs. 'As to the rest, I've seen him with the nurses when he's come to visit me… They all think the world of him and the single ones are ripe for the picking. I really like him but I don't want to see you get hurt.'

A quick stab of jealousy lanced through Caitlin at the mention of the nurses, but just then a bout of coughing caught her mother out. Caitlin stood up and quickly handed her the oxygen mask that was connected to the wall-mounted delivery system close by.

'Here, breathe in slowly, steadily. Take your time.'

After a few minutes her mother was feeling better and she put the mask aside. 'I'm fine now,' she said. 'I just need to rest for a bit.'

Caitlin nodded, giving her an assessing look. 'Okay. I should be getting back to work, anyway. I've a new patient coming in and I need to look her over.' She gently squeezed her hand. 'I'll be back to see you later.'

She went back to the children's unit, pleased to see that a trio of small children who were able to get out of bed for short periods had gathered around the brand-new aquarium tank that Brodie had introduced to the ward. They were pointing, talking and smiling a lot.

'I see your tropical fish tank is a hit with the youngsters,' she told Brodie at the desk as she read through her patient's file.

He smiled. 'Yes, I noticed one or two of them going up to the glass and watching what was going on. They seem to like the shipwreck and submerged treasure chest, and the fish are colourful.' He brought up some CT scans on the computer screen. 'The next step for me, I think, is to develop a rehab garden outside so that children like Jason and maybe Sammy, who are recovering, can get their strength back by walking about outside on good days.'

'That sounds like an interesting idea.' She looked at him curiously. 'What did you have in mind?'

'Different levels. Nothing too high but raised flower beds, pathways, short flights of wide steps—providing the children have physiotherapists or parents with them to help them negotiate the obstacles. I thought maybe scented flowers and herbs, or different colours and textures, would go down well.'

'Something to attract wildlife, like birds and squirrels, would be good,' she said. 'So maybe you could put up a bird table and plant a variety of shrubs that have the right kind of berries.' She broke off, studying him once more. 'I think you have some great ideas, but where's the funding coming from?'

'There are hospital charities keen on helping out,' he answered. 'And I'll think about putting some of my own money into it. It all depends if I decide to stay here for the long term.'

She frowned at that. Was he really thinking of moving on?

He brought up X-ray films on to the screen of his computer then he frowned and pointed to the images. 'Have you seen these?'

'No. Whose are they?'

'They're films we had done recently to check

Sammy's progress. Along with the results of his DNA and collagen tests, I think we finally have an answer. We're dealing with a specific bone disease—*osteogenesis imperfecta.'*

She winced. 'Poor Sammy,' she said softly. The diagnosis, otherwise known as brittle bone disease, meant that his body didn't make enough collagen—the main protein building block of bone—so his bones and connective tissue, such as tendons and ligaments would suffer as a result. 'So his bones are thin and liable to break more easily than others.' She studied the films on screen carefully. 'It's difficult to detect from the X-rays alone.'

'But the bones are definitely thinner than normal—perhaps his case is mild and he's been unfortunate up to now.'

'Well, let's hope so. The physiotherapist is working with him because of the fracture but it'll be good for him to have ongoing therapy to help him regain his strength and mobility—safe exercise and activity to develop his muscle control.'

He nodded. 'His parents will need advice on nutrition—we can't replace the collagen, but we can make sure his muscles and bones are as strong as possible. Bisphosphonates are the mainstay of drug treatment as far as that goes.'

'I'll get things organised.' She gave a faint smile. 'The one good thing to come out of the diagnosis is that it means the parents are off the hook. It's going to be difficult for them to take it on board—a bittersweet experience.'

'But they'll have an answer at last and so will Social Services and the police.'

'Yes.' Caitlin hurried away to make several phone
calls and to get the next phase of Sammy's treatment
started. This was a case where she didn't want to waste
any time. The parents had been weighed down by
doubt, uncertainty and recriminations for long enough;
perhaps now Sammy would truly start to make a recovery. It was hardly any wonder the child was quiet
and withdrawn.

The rest of the day passed quickly. A little girl,
Janine, was admitted with an infection and Caitlin
ordered tests to find out what they were dealing with.
'I'll prescribe a broad-spectrum antibiotic,' she told the
staff nurse. 'But when we get the results back from the
lab we can prescribe a more specific drug.'

'Okay, I'll see to it,' the staff nurse said.

'Thanks.'

When her shift ended Caitlin was more anxious than
usual to get home. Brodie came out of one of the bays
where he had been examining a child and sent her a
quick glance as she went to collect her jacket. 'You're
off home, then? You look anxious. Are you worried
about Daisy?'

She nodded. 'I am, a bit. Rosie's mother phoned to
say Daisy was quite restless, so I'm expecting things
to kick off any time soon.'

'I'll come and join you as soon as I finish here. I
could pick up a Chinese takeaway on my way home,
if you want? I know you like it and that'll be one less
chore.'

'Ah, my favourite food...' she said with a smile. 'Beef and green peppers in black bean sauce—yum— and sweet-and-sour chicken. Oh, I'm hungry already at the thought of it.'

'Me too.' He said it softly, his gaze moving over her, lingering; somehow she had the feeling his mind wasn't simply dwelling on the prospect of food.

It was only after she'd left the hospital and was driving home along the country lanes that she wondered about the wisdom of spending too many of her evenings with him, especially this evening, when they were planning to share a mutual treat. It was one thing to throw a sandwich together out of expediency— quite another to make a date. Because that was what it seemed like, all at once. Things were moving too fast. It wasn't too long ago that she'd been looking forward to spending her free time with Matt and look where that had left her. She frowned. What was it about Matt that had made her think he was the one for her, when he so obviously wasn't?

Brodie turned up at the house a couple of hours later as dusk was falling. Caitlin had been watering the plants in the kitchen garden but now she turned off the tap and put the hose away.

'How is Daisy?' Brodie asked. 'Is anything happening with her?'

Caitlin nodded. 'She's definitely not herself. She's a bit agitated, so I brought her into the house—she's in the utility room. Her bed fits in there nicely under the worktop, and it's shaded from the sun during the daytime. She seems to like it there, anyway, so I'll probably let her stay. I left her rearranging her blanket. Come and see.'

She led the way into the house and Brodie put his packages down on the kitchen table. The appetising smell of Chinese food wafted on the air.

She hastily set plates to warm in the oven and then they looked in on Daisy. She looked up at them from her bed, panting, her tongue lolling eagerly.

'She looks happy enough, anyway,' Brodie commented, stroking the dog's head then heading back towards the kitchen. He washed his hands at the sink then helped Caitlin to set out the food.

'Has David said anything more about the filming?' Caitlin asked a while later as she nibbled on a hot spring roll.

He nodded. 'It's all going to start in a couple of days—they have the weekend marked up for it. He's even roped Dad in. Heaven knows how he managed it, but he's going to be kitted out as a farm worker, by all accounts.'

'You're kidding?' It was hard to believe that Colin Driscoll would ever have agreed to it. 'How do you feel about that?'

He lifted his shoulders briefly. 'I'm not sure. I suppose anything that gets us together is a good thing. We're both adults now and it's about time we sorted out our differences. He may not have wanted me around, but he brought me up from when I was a baby, so you'd think he'd have found some feelings for me along the way.'

He frowned. 'But then things happened... I started

acting up, and after I turned eighteen I stayed away, just coming back to see David whenever I could. It seemed for the best.' He raised his dark brows a fraction. 'Maybe, after all this time, Dad might be able to come to terms with the circumstances and finally find acceptance, though I think that's a tall order—for both of us.'

Caitlin mused on that. 'He was never the easiest man to get along with. Not in later years, anyway. He'd come over here to buy produce from my mother, but he was often brusque, and wouldn't want to stay and chat.' She dipped her fork into delicious fried rice and said thoughtfully, 'Have you tried to find your real father?'

He nodded. 'There's no father named on my birth certificate. Dad said he was a Londoner, someone who was setting up his own business, but he didn't know his surname or very much about him. I think he and Mum made some kind of pact not to talk about him. So finding him has always seemed like a non-starter.'

'I'm sorry. I can't imagine what that must be like, not knowing your parents.'

'You learn to live with it.' He speared a tender shoot of broccoli and rolled it around in the spicy sauce. 'There's always a part of you that's missing; when you do something or think something odd or slightly different from usual, you wonder if that's come from your absent parent. Genetics suddenly seem ultra-important, but there's not a thing you can do to find out the truth, so you have no choice but to bury the frustration inside.'

'David says you can't settle and you can't move on—

perhaps, like your dad, you need to find acceptance of some sort.'

He gave a short laugh. 'That's easy to say but not so easy to do in practice. David knows who he is, where he comes from. He's content with his life as it is. It's reasonably orderly and he doesn't need to think too deeply about what he wants from life. He assumes he'll have a great time now and settle down when he finds the right person. He seems to be fairly certain that will happen some day; I'm glad for him.'

'But you're not so clear about that for yourself?'

He shook his head. 'I've seen how people mess things up—I'm a direct result of that—and I don't want to be part of causing it to happen to anyone else. Perhaps I don't believe in the happy-ever-after. I wish I did. I wish it was possible.' He sent her a quick, almost regretful glance. 'For myself, I think I prefer to live in the here and now, and take things as I find them. If I can have fun along the way, that's great, but I don't make any long-term plans because I don't know what's around the corner.'

'That's what you were trying to tell me the other day, isn't it? I shouldn't look for anything more from you.' She studied him, her grey eyes solemn. 'I'm sorry about that—I can't help thinking it's a pity you can't put as much meaning into your personal life as you do into your work.'

He gave her a rueful smile. 'You're right. I do concentrate most of my energy in my work. That's important to me.' He frowned. 'I can't seem to help myself,

Caitlin. Maybe I don't want to think too deeply about anything else.'

'I thought that might be the reason.' Her mouth turned downwards briefly. 'But I suppose all the hard work is paying dividends. I've seen what you've managed to achieve at the hospital. The patients are well looked after, the parents are fully involved in their care and the staff are focused. I'm not surprised you've become head of a unit so early in your career.' She sent him a quizzical glance. 'This won't be your last stop, will it? You'll do what you need to do here and then move on to improve things at some other hospital.'

His blue gaze meshed with hers. 'I don't know about that. Right now I'm concentrating on the job here.'

They finished their meal and went to check on Daisy. There had been no sound coming from the utility room but now, as they looked in on the dog, they heard soft licking noises.

'Oh, my word, look at that!' Caitlin gasped as she saw two wriggling, sleek little puppies suckling at their mother's teats. Too busy to notice that she had visitors, Daisy was intent on licking them clean and only stopped when a third pup began to put in an appearance.

'Well, who's a clever girl?' Brodie grinned as he knelt down beside the dog bed. 'Look at you—you've managed it all by yourself.' Caitlin crouched down beside him and he put his arm around her, drawing her close. 'She's a natural,' he said. 'And there was me

thinking we might have to help out, or call the vet if
she got into difficulties.'

Caitlin was overwhelmed as she watched Daisy de-
liver a fourth then a fifth puppy, all perfect, all hungry and vying for a place where they could suckle.
'It's wonderful,' she said, thrilled to bits to see that
they were all healthy and strong looking. She turned
her head to look at Brodie and he smiled back at her.

'It is,' he agreed. He moved closer to her so that his
lips were just a breath away from hers—then he kissed
her, hard and fast, a thorough, satisfying kiss. She was
so taken by surprise and caught up in the joy of everything that was going on that she kissed him back,
loving the feel of his arms around her, loving the fact
that they'd shared this momentous occasion together.

They kissed and held on to each other for what
seemed like a blissful eternity, until there was a sharp
rapping at the kitchen door and David was calling out,
'Anyone at home? Caitlin? Brodie?'

They broke away from one another as they heard
the outer door open; David stepped inside the kitchen
and came looking for them. Sure that her cheeks were
flushed with heat, Caitlin looked back at the dog and
her wriggling pups.

'We're in here,' Brodie said. 'We've had some new
additions to the family.'

'Hey, that's great.' David came to look at the proud
mother, kneeling down to stroke her gently and admire
her offspring. 'Well done, Daisy. Are you all done,
now? Is that it…five altogether? Wow!'

They watched the tableau for a while and then David

asked, 'Is that Chinese food going spare in the kitchen? Only, I haven't eaten for hours.'

'Help yourself.' Caitlin stood up. 'I'll get you a plate.'

'Cheers. You're an angel,' David murmured. 'Oh, and at the weekend, I thought you might want to play the part of a farm girl feeding the hens—Brodie can be hoeing the kitchen garden. I talked it over with the producer and he's okay with that. You don't have to say anything, just do the actions.'

Brodie followed them into the kitchen, frowning. 'So what's the scene all about?'

David took a seat at the table and helped himself to stir-fried noodles and chicken. 'It'll be mostly centred around the barn—the detective is looking for a suspect and asks the farmer if anyone's been hiding out in the barn overnight. The farmer says no, but then they find a bloodstain in the straw and after that the forensic team is brought in.'

'That's it?' Brodie raised his brows expressively.

'Yeah. It's an essential part of the drama. Someone was there, see, but the body has been moved.'

'The plot thickens.' Caitlin chuckled. 'What does your father have to do in the scene?'

'He'll be delivering foodstuff for the animals— unloading it off a lorry. I suppose Brodie could go and give him a hand—yeah, that would be good. It'll fit in with the red herring we planned: he looks like the man who drove the getaway car—our prime suspect.'

Caitlin smiled. 'What a pity the drama spans the TV watershed; the youngsters in the children's unit will be missing a treat—their favourite doctor on TV. Unless, of course, their parents let them stay up for the first half.'

Brodie's eyes narrowed on her. 'Please don't tell them. I'll never hear the last of it.'

She chuckled, but David said quickly, 'I think most people roundabout will know, sooner or later. The press will be on hand for the filming—you know the sort of thing: "*Murder Mysteries* will be back on your screens for the autumn. Filming is taking place now in the peaceful, picturesque village of Ashley Vale, Buckinghamshire. Local doctors have given over their properties for the recording..."'

Brodie groaned. 'Why did I ever agree to this? We'll have the local newshounds all over us as well as the national.'

Caitlin lightly patted his shoulder. 'Look on the bright side: you'll be out at work most of the time. Unless they follow you and find you there, of course...'

He groaned again, louder this time, and they laughed.

The film crew arrived early in the morning on Saturday to allow time for costume, make-up and setting the scene. David had the bright idea of putting Daisy and her puppies in a wooden feed trough in the barn. They would be written into the scene, he said—a means whereby the victim of the story was drawn to the barn. 'It'll be a sweet moment in the drama,' he said, 'Seeing them all golden-haired and snuggled together.' They were certainly thriving, getting bigger every day.

Dressed in jeans and a T-shirt, Caitlin duly went out to scatter corn for the hens. There was a moment of aggravation when the geese decided they needed to ward off the visitors, but after a few minutes of chasing about, she and Brodie managed to grab hold of them and shut them in one of the outhouses.

'I'll give them a feed of leftover vegetables and pellets to keep them happy,' Caitlin said, breathless after her exertions. 'I hope we haven't disrupted the filming too much.'

'I think they're used to happenings like that on set,' Brodie murmured. 'Besides, it's given you quite a glow—you'll look great on camera.'

So she was flushed and harassed already—not a good start. One of the extras was wheezing heavily as he walked by the barn to the lorry but she decided perhaps that was the part he was meant to play. Anyway, Brodie was with him, unloading sacks of grain, his shirt sleeves rolled up, biceps bulging.

She looked away, her own lungs unexpectedly dysfunctional all of a sudden. She began to spread corn over the ground, trying not to show that she'd been affected in any way by his sheer animal magnetism.

For his part, Brodie's father stood by the lorry and helped to unload the sacks. He and Brodie spoke briefly to one another in undertones as they worked, but their expressions were taut, businesslike. Brodie heaved another sack from the lorry and walked with it on his shoulder to the barn.

'Okay, thanks, everyone. That's a wrap on this scene!' the director said after a while. He went over to the film crew. 'We'll move on down the lane in half an hour and do the accident scene. David, you need to come along with us—I'm not sure the script works too well where the policewoman finds the overturned car with the woman at the wheel. She's on her way to meet her daughter at the farm but I'm not sure her feelings of anxiety are fully shown. Maybe you can tighten it up a bit.'

'Okay.' David winced briefly but he didn't seem too bothered by the request and Caitlin guessed he was used to being asked to make last-minute changes.

'An overturned car?' Brodie shot David a piercing look. 'You didn't mention that part of the script when you told me about the episode.'

David pulled a face. 'It was something the producer wanted written in to heighten the drama. There are only the main members of the cast involved, so I didn't think you'd need to know the details.'

Brodie's expression was taut. 'Don't you have any problem with it?'

David's mouth flattened. 'Of course I do—but it's my job, Brodie. I don't have a choice but to go along with things. You understand that, don't you?'

Brodie didn't answer. His jaw flexed and his eyes glittered, bleak and as hard as flint.

Caitlin watched them, two brothers deep in earnest conversation, and knew something was badly wrong. A car accident had featured heavily in their young lives—it had been the cause of major tragedy for both of them. Was that what was causing the tension between them now?

David glanced at her. 'I should have said something before this,' he murmured. 'It was bound to come as a shock…a reminder of what happened. I've had time to get used to it because I've been working on the original script for some weeks.' The director was on the move, briskly calling for the crew to follow him, and David looked back at his brother. 'I have to go. Will you be all right?'

'Of course.' Brodie's answer was curt but David clearly wasn't convinced. Once more, he looked at Caitlin and made a helpless gesture with his hands.

She gave an imperceptible nod. 'Brodie, let's go and get a coffee, shall we? And I need to let the geese out of prison as soon as the crew have gone.'

'They're all packing up and moving out along the lane. It shouldn't take them too long. I imagine it will be safe soon enough.' He walked over to the barn, calling out, 'I'll get Daisy and her brood.'

His father had already left, Caitlin noticed, and she wondered if that bothered him too. She'd invited Colin to stay behind for coffee and a snack earlier, but he'd declined the offer, saying he had to get back to Mill House. He was having problems with his roof.

Brodie installed Daisy and the puppies—three male, two female—back in their new home in the utility room and then came into the kitchen. Caitlin poured coffee into a mug and slid it across the table towards him. 'I see you let the geese out,' she murmured, glancing through the kitchen window. 'They've taken up position by the gate, just in case anyone tries to come back.'

He made a faint smile at that. 'It's good to know we

don't need a guard dog. I'm not sure Daisy would be up to the job right now.'

'I don't know about that. Wait till the pups are wandering about. I expect she'll be very protective of them—the mothering instinct will take over.'

Brodie's expression tautened and she quickly sat down opposite him at the table, placing her hand over his in a comforting gesture. 'What's wrong, Brodie? Do you want to tell me about it?'

'Nothing's wrong.' He stiffened, sitting straight backed, his gaze dark.

'Your mood changed as soon as you heard about the car scene. Perhaps it will help to talk about it.'

'I don't see how. Anyway, it was all a long time ago. It shouldn't...' His voice trailed off and Caitlin gently ran her hand over his.

'Did you ever talk about what happened? This is about your mother, isn't it? Why don't you bring it out into the open once and for all? Tell me what you're thinking. It might help.'

Angry sparks flared in his eyes. 'Don't you think David suffered just as much as I did? He lost her too, you know, and he was younger than me. She was a huge loss to all of us.'

'I know. But there's something that's been burning inside you ever since it happened. I saw it in your face after the accident. I knew there was something you weren't telling me...something you kept locked up inside. What is it, Brodie? Why can't you tell me what's wrong?'

He wrapped his hands around his coffee cup and

pulled in a deep breath, bending his head so that she wouldn't see his face. When he spoke, finally, it was almost a whisper. 'It was my fault,' he said.

She frowned. 'How could it be your fault? You weren't there. It was dark and there was a rainstorm—the roads were treacherous. She went into a skid on a bend in a country lane and the car overturned. How was that your fault? How could you even think it?'

'I was sixteen. I'd stayed out too long in town—way past when I was supposed to be home—and the buses weren't running. I didn't have the money for a taxi, so I phoned home and asked for a lift.'

His voice was low so she strained to hear what he was saying. He took a shuddery breath and went on, 'Dad answered the phone. He was furious because I'd been irresponsible and he told me to walk home in the rain. It was twelve miles, and I argued with him, kicked up a fuss, which made him worse. He was going to put the phone down on me but my mother came on the line and wanted to know where I was. She came out to fetch me because he refused.'

His hands clenched into fists. 'It was my fault she died,' he said. 'I should have walked home. In the end, the police came and found me and told me what had happened. My dad didn't speak to me for days.'

A small gasp escaped her. 'I didn't know…about the row, I mean. I'm so sorry, Brodie.' She stood up and put her arms around him. 'It was an awful thing to happen, but it wasn't your fault. Lots of teenagers get into scrapes and cause their parents hassle. You can't go on blaming yourself.'

'But I do.' He pulled a face. 'Logically, I know all the reasoning, the explanations—but in my heart I feel the guilt all the time. I don't feel I have the right to be happy. I didn't know how to handle it when I was younger, but later I decided to try to make some kind of reparation by going into medicine. It doesn't appease my guilt but it helps, a bit.'

'Believe me, you've done everything you can. And now you have to put it behind you. Your mother wouldn't want you to go on blaming yourself. She wouldn't want you to waste your life feeling guilty.'

His brow creased. 'No, perhaps not.'

'Definitely not. She was always there for you, Brodie. She loved you. She would want you to be happy. And I think she would have wanted you to make up with your dad.'

She rested her cheek against his. 'She would have hated the way your father reacted afterwards, not speaking to you, but have you ever thought that maybe, once he was over the initial shock, that he felt guilty too? You asked him to come and get you and he refused—maybe, if he'd been driving, he'd have handled the road conditions differently. Perhaps that's why you and he can't get on—you both feel that you're equally to blame for what happened.'

He sighed heavily. 'I know... I know...you're probably right. I've been over and over it in my mind. But I don't see how we can resolve things after all this time. I stayed away because I wasn't wanted but now I've come back here to work, he does his best to avoid me.'

'Does he? Are you sure about that?' She straightened, letting her arms fall to her sides. 'Why did he take part in the filming today? He didn't have to do it. He could have found an excuse and stayed away. But he didn't, Brodie. He came along, knowing you would be here. It isn't much, but it's a start. Don't you agree?'

'I suppose so.' His mouth made a crooked, awkward line. 'The truth is, I'm not actually sure I want to make up with my dad. He treated me harshly and it left a scar.'

'You've both been scarred. It's time to start the healing process.'

He gave her a long, assessing look. 'When all's said and done, I think that's what I like about you, Caity. You've always made me look at the big picture, made me face up to what I'm doing with my life; shown me what a mess I'm making...even if it's not what I want to know at the time.'

'Maybe I do it because I care about you,' she said softly. 'I don't think you're making a mess of things—you're doing the best you can in the circumstances. I want to help you. I don't want to see you hurting.'

And maybe she did it because she loved him... because she'd always loved him, though she hadn't always recognised it.

His revelations had shocked her to the core, but now she understood why he had so many doubts about himself. Perhaps this tragedy of his childhood, together with the uncertainty of his parentage and the difficult relationship with his father, were all part of the reason why he couldn't commit to love.

For herself, she had come to realise that her feelings

for him went very deep, far more than she had allowed herself to acknowledge until this moment. He might not feel the same way about her, didn't even know what he wanted right now, but she would look out for him all the same. She couldn't help herself.

CHAPTER SIX

'I HAVE TO go over to the hospital to deal with a couple of things that have cropped up,' Brodie said. It was Sunday morning; he'd surprised Caitlin by appearing on her doorstep some time after breakfast.

She was dressed casually in a short-sleeved shirt and pencil-line skirt that faithfully outlined her curves. She was inwardly thrilled that he appeared totally distracted for a moment as he looked at her, until he shook his head, as though to clear it.

'Uh, something…something's happened with one of your patients—a reaction to the medication she was prescribed—and I wondered if you want to come with me. It's Janine, the five-year-old with the chest infection.'

'Heavens, yes, of course I'll come with you.' She was appalled by the news and immediately on the alert. 'Is she all right?'

'I believe so. It looks as though she's allergic to the penicillin she was given this morning. Her throat swelled up, she was wheezing and she has an all-over rash. The registrar acted quickly to put things right, but obviously the parents are upset, so I want to go and talk to them.'

'Okay.' She made sure Daisy and the puppies were safely ensconced in the utility room and grabbed her jacket, going out with him to his car.

The roads were fairly clear of traffic but Brodie drove carefully as usual and appeared to be deep in thought. 'You're very quiet,' she commented. 'Are you worried about the situation at the hospital?'

He shook his head. 'These things happen. It's no one's fault, and the little girl is all right.'

'Okay.' She glanced at him, noting the straight line of his mouth. Was he dwelling on what they'd talked about yesterday, about his problems with his father? 'Is it your dad, then? Are you going to try to sort things out with him this afternoon when the film crew set up again?'

He shrugged. 'I haven't given it much thought. I prefer not to think about it.'

It was clear he wasn't going to talk about it and she was disappointed. Maybe that was selfish on her part, but she couldn't help feeling that sorting out the problems from his past was the key to his chance of true happiness for the future.

Would that future include her? Something in her desperately wanted to keep him in her life but, at this point in time, who could tell if it would come about? More importantly, would any relationship last? He had more than enough problems to overcome and, as for herself, she'd been through a lot of heartache; she didn't want to put herself through any more. Caring had been her downfall. Somehow, she had to be strong, put up defences and guard herself against being hurt.

And right now they both had more pressing matters to deal with. Of course he was right to stay focused.

At the hospital, Brodie showed Janine's distraught parents into his office and invited them to make themselves comfortable in the upholstered chairs. The room was designed to put people at ease—carpeted underfoot and fitted out with pale gold beechwood furniture.

'Unfortunately, Janine had an allergic reaction to the penicillin,' he told them. 'It's fairly unusual, but luckily the doctor on duty caught it quickly and gave her an injection of adrenaline. We'll give her steroid medication as well for a short time, and obviously she needs to have a different antibiotic.' He frowned. 'The allergy wasn't noted before this on her records, so I'm assuming this is the first time she's had a reaction like that?' He looked at the parents for confirmation.

The girl's mother nodded. 'She's always been healthy up to now and not needed penicillin. We were just so shocked when we saw what was happening to her.'

'That's understandable.' Brodie was sympathetic.

'I'm so sorry this happened to her,' Caitlin said. 'We hoped that the penicillin would resolve the problem of her infection but clearly she'll need to avoid it in any form from now on.'

'We'll inform her GP,' Brodie said. 'And a note will be made in the records. This shouldn't happen again but you'll need to tell any medical practitioner of the allergy if they plan on prescribing antibiotics for her.'

'We'll do that,' the father said. 'Thank you both for taking the trouble to come and talk to us. It's been a worrying time.'

'I know it must have been very distressing for you,' Brodie said. 'But I've spoken to the registrar and you can be reassured that Janine is all right. She won't suffer any long-lasting effects and the rash will fade in a couple or so days.'

They spoke for a little while longer then, as they were leaving the office, the staff nurse took Caitlin to one side. 'I have a mother here who is worried about her baby,' she said quietly. 'Seeing that you're here, would you have a word with her?'

'Of course.'

'You might as well use my office,' Brodie said. He lightly touched her arm in a gesture of reassurance. 'I expect this thing with the mother is something you can sort out easily enough.'

Caitlin hoped so too.

'I have to go and meet up with my animal therapy volunteer,' Brodie said. 'She rang me earlier to say she'd like to come in—but I'll catch up with you later.'

'Okay.'

The nurse handed her the baby's thin file and she skimmed the notes quickly. By the time the young mother arrived at the office with the infant in her arms, she was fully prepared.

'How can I help you?' she asked with a smile, inviting her to sit down in a comfy armchair.

'It's just that the surgeon tried to explain things to me, but I don't really understand what's happening to my baby.' The young mother held her baby close to her, wrapping her more firmly in her shawl and looking anxiously at Caitlin. 'Olivia's only five weeks old— she keeps being sick and she's losing weight. I'm really worried about her. Why can't she keep her milk down?'

'I know this is upsetting for you, but really, it's a simple, straightforward operation,' Caitlin answered kindly. 'I'll get some paper and a pen and see if I can draw it for you.'

Swiftly, she drew the outline of a baby's stomach, showing the opening into the intestine. 'Usually, see, the opening is wide enough to let the milk pass through—but sometimes the muscle here is thick and causes a blockage. When that happens, the milk can't get from the stomach to the intestine and the baby brings it back up. It's a forceful, projectile vomiting, as you've discovered, rather than a gentle regurgitation of excess milk.'

'How will the surgeon put it right? Is it a big operation? Will it leave a scar?'

'The incision will be very small, near the belly button, and there shouldn't be much of a scar at all, once it's all healed up. The surgeon will cut the muscle and that will cause the opening to be wider.'

'Okay, I get that, I think.' The young woman frowned. 'The doctor said she would be admitted to hospital today but they wouldn't operate until tomorrow. What does it mean? Will you be doing tests and so on?'

'Mainly for the next few hours we'll be making sure that she's not dehydrated—that's our biggest concern, so she'll have a fluid line inserted in a vein. It won't hurt her, but the repeated vomiting means she's lost a lot of fluid and it needs to be put right, along with minute traces of sodium and potassium and so on that might be out of balance. We'll need to do some blood tests to check that all's well.'

'All right.' The woman nodded, seemingly reassured. 'Thanks for explaining it to me.' She gently rocked the baby in her arms, soothing her. 'How long will she need to be in hospital?'

'Until about two or three days after the surgery to make sure she's feeding properly and that her temperature and blood pressure and so on are normal.'

The girl looked troubled. 'Will I be able to stay with her?'

'Yes, we have a room where you can sleep and still be close to Olivia. The nurse will show you where you can put your things—and if you think of any more questions, just ask. We're all happy to help.'

'Thanks.'

A nurse came to show her where the baby would be looked after and Caitlin, relieved that she'd been able to help, went in search of Brodie. He was in one of the patients' bays.

He smiled as Caitlin entered the room. A woman was with him, a slim, middle-aged woman with a kindly face, and she had a calm-looking yellow Labrador on a lead by her side.

Caitlin watched as the woman introduced the dog to the children. They patted and stroked him and Brodie was smiling, looking totally relaxed. Maybe a dog was good therapy for Brodie too, she mused.

'He's like a giant, cuddly teddy bear,' Jason said, laughing in delight. The four-year-old was getting on well now, off the oxygen for the most part, but having brief sessions with the nebuliser every few hours. He was sitting in the chair by his bed with his parents looking on.

The other little boy, Sammy, two years old and still with his leg in a cast, was much more reticent. He was in hospital briefly for further tests. He too was seated; now he cautiously reached out to touch the dog's head but pulled his hand back when the dog turned to look at him with big, brown eyes.

'It's all right, he won't hurt you,' the dog's owner told him. 'He loves children and he likes being stroked.' She crouched down to his level and demonstrated.

Sammy seemed to take to her. 'What's his name?' he asked in a timid voice.

'Well, we call him Toffee, because he's such a gorgeous toffee colour. I think it suits him, don't you?'

Sammy giggled. 'Toffee,' he said and giggled again. 'Toffee…' He bent over, laughing, as if he found that hilariously funny. Recovering himself, he looked at the Labrador once more and tentatively reached out to stroke him. 'Toffee's a sweetie, what you eat,' he said, chuckling.

Toffee's owner smiled and Sammy's mother said cheerfully, 'Well, he is a bit of a sweetie, isn't he? He's lovely.' She looked at the woman and then at Brodie. 'I'm so glad you brought him in to see us. It's been the best thing for Sammy—for Jason too, from the looks of things.'

Both boys were patting the dog now, their troubles forgotten for the time being. Caitlin relaxed, seeing her young charges happy and on the mend.

'That worked out really well,' she commented to Brodie when they went for lunch in the cafeteria. 'I'm glad we came in this morning.'

'So am I. Anyway, I wanted to be here when the dog was brought in. I think he'll be a great hit with the children. He certainly brought Sammy out of his shell.'

'He did. We'll have to try the dog with children who are in wheelchairs—there won't be any danger of them being accidentally nudged and he'll cheer them up no end.' They filled their trays with a Sunday roast dinner—beef, Yorkshire puddings with roast potatoes and an assortment of vegetables—and went to sit at a table in the far corner of the room.

Brodie glanced at Caitlin as he started to eat. 'I meant to tell you, I heard from Matt the other day.' His gaze was thoughtful, pondering. 'He phoned.'

'Oh yes?' She stared at him, suddenly very still.

'He's been back at work for a while now and he was asking about you. He wondered how you were doing.' She nodded slowly, taking that in, and he went on, 'He said to tell you the little boy you were treating—the one with the infection in his knee—is completely better now and fully mobile. He came to the outpatients' clinic the other day.'

'I'm glad about that.' Molly must have told him she wanted to follow up on the boy. She looked at Brodie guardedly. Matt hadn't phoned only to update her, had he? 'What did you say to him?'

He lifted a dark brow in query. 'About how you were doing?'

She nodded, not trusting herself to speak. She hadn't thought about Matt recently but now, at the mention of him, her palms were clammy and her mouth was dry. Her hand trembled a little so she laid down her fork and rested her fingers beside her plate. Brodie's blue eyes followed the action.

'I told him you were doing fine—no thanks to him, since he'd treated you so badly.'

She gave a small gasp. 'You said that? But Brodie, he's your friend…'

He shrugged. 'I couldn't say too much to him about it at the wedding—it was the wrong time—but I wanted him to know that I didn't like the way he'd behaved towards you.'

She shook her head. 'You shouldn't have done that— it was between me and him.'

His blue gaze was steady. 'He was my friend, yes, my best friend, so I could be straight with him. I didn't like it in the first place when I heard he'd started dating you; all kinds of bad feelings swept over me… jealousy, for the most part…but when he took up with Jenny I had mixed feelings. I was glad it was over between you because it meant you were free—but I was concerned for you.'

Her eyes widened a fraction. He'd been jealous? 'I'd no idea you were keeping tabs on me.'

'I've often enquired after you—talked to people

I know, kept in touch with your mother from time to time.' His mouth flattened. 'Anyway, I told Matt you were getting on well in your new job, that it was great living next door to you and I wished I'd moved in sooner. It's all true, of course.' His gaze meshed with hers.

She smiled faintly at his admission. It made her feel better, knowing he liked being near to her, and she expelled her breath in a soft sigh. 'I thought I was in love with him, that we would get married, but I had it all wrong, didn't I? How is it possible to make a mistake like that? It's left me so that I don't know if I can trust my feelings any more.'

'Yes, I know. But you could have ended up in a bad marriage. So maybe you had a lucky escape.'

She tried a smile. 'Then again, we could have been okay. Marriage is what you make it. It depends what you put into it.'

He shook his head. 'You'd both have had to work at it, and Matt obviously wasn't prepared to do that. Something must have been out of sync for him to go off with Jenny the way he did.'

'Yes, you pointed that out once before.' She pressed her lips together, trying not to let her emotions show. After all this time she was still on fragile ground, and she sensed that Brodie was pushing things, testing her to see if she would stumble.

'Have you given it any thought?'

She nodded. 'I have but I'm still not exactly sure what happened,' she said cautiously. 'All I can think is...' She took a deep breath. 'I've always tried to handle situations by myself the best way I can. Ever since my dad died, I've tried to be independent, to make sure Mum was all right. But Jenny was never like that. She needed help—with her car, with her state of mind. Things had gone wrong for her and she was a damsel in distress. She's often needy and I think that must have appealed to Matt. Perhaps he needs to be with some-one who will rely on him for support. She brings out the protector in him, whereas I… Perhaps I don't have that same vulnerability.'

Brodie mulled it over as he slid his fork into green beans. 'I don't know about that—the vulnerability thing. I'd want to make sure you were okay, no matter what.' He ate thoughtfully for a second or two. 'You could be right, though. Matt does tend to want to take control.' He studied her as she picked up her own fork once more and began to eat. 'He's a fool, if he doesn't see what he let go.'

'Thanks for that. But perhaps it was for the best. I suppose it wouldn't have worked out for us in the end. I wouldn't want to be in a bad marriage. My parents were always good together, and their kind of relation-ship is what I want for myself.'

'I can understand that. That's probably why I've never felt the urge to try it. I don't want to make a mis-take like my mother did with my real, my natural, fa-ther and then again with my dad. If it had been a good marriage, he would have handled things differently.'

'Perhaps…but they stayed together, so they must have had something pretty strong going for them.'

He seemed to be mulling that over. 'I suppose so. I've been looking at things from a different angle.'

She tasted the medium-rare roast beef, savouring it for a moment on her tongue. His troubled background would always affect the way he felt about relationships. 'Obviously, when it comes to marriage, you're afraid,' she said eventually. 'That's why you flit from woman to woman without making any commitments.'

His eyes narrowed in mock jest. 'Who's been talking?'

She gave a wry smile. 'My mother, for one, and the hospital grapevine is rife with rumour as usual.'

He laid down his fork. 'Your mother I can't account for, and I won't argue with her because I'm really very fond of her. But I can tell you now that whatever you've heard on the grapevine is pure conjecture. I haven't dated anyone since I came back to Ashley Vale.'

She looked at him steadily. 'Maybe you've been too busy.'

He gave a short laugh, returning her gaze with a penetrating blue glance. 'Yes, maybe. Perhaps I've found someone special…someone who cares about me and makes me feel I might actually be worthy.'

The breath caught in her throat as she met his gaze. If only she could believe what he was saying. 'That sounds…wonderful…something to be working on.'

'I'm glad you think so.' Smiling, he returned his attention to his meal.

Caitlin finished her main course and reached for her dessert, a Bramley apple pie topped with creamy custard. She didn't know what to think. He was making

out he was perfectly innocent but she knew him of old.
He was a wolf in sheep's clothing. He would lure her
into a false sense of security then when she was completely ensnared he would devour her and move on in
search of new prey. Didn't she know better than to fall
for his charm? She'd already been hurt badly by Matt.
She was feeling stronger now but surely she shouldn't
make herself vulnerable again if she could help it? All
the same, she was so, so tempted.

'Hey, you two, have you seen the pictures in the papers? You've even made the nationals—look.'

Cathy, the staff nurse from the children's unit, came
over to their table. 'Am I interrupting?'

'No, of course not,' Caitlin said. 'Are these the pictures from *Murder Mysteries*?'

Cathy nodded. 'Yes, look. I bought the local paper
and the *Tribune*. You're both splashed over the TV
feature pages—it's mostly the main characters they're
showing, but you two are there as well. I can't wait to
see the series when it comes out. I'll be watching out
for your scenes all the way through.'

Caitlin and Brodie glanced through the papers. 'Oh,'
Caitlin said, 'They filmed the geese when they ran
up to the camera!' Brodie was in the shot, smiling as
he looked at the startled cameraman. 'I thought they
would edit those shots.'

'They probably have in the TV version—but the
press will choose whatever appeals, I suppose.' Brodie was amused. 'Thanks for showing us these, Cathy.'

'You're welcome. I expect they're in all the papers.
All the nurses are talking about them.'

She went off to join her friends, leaving Caitlin and Brodie to finish their lunch. Afterwards, they went to spend some time with Caitlin's mother.

'The doctor says I should be well enough to leave here in a few days,' her mother said, looking happy. Her cheeks were flushed with anticipation. 'I'm so pleased. I can't wait.'

'It'll be good to have you home,' Caitlin said, giving her a hug.

They stayed for half an hour then left to meet up with the film crew once more back at the smallholding. David was already there, organising things. Caitlin had given him access to the house and grounds.

'I thought Daisy and her puppies would like to be out in the sunshine for a bit,' he said, coming over to greet them, 'so I've put them on the lawn. They won't be going anywhere,' he added with a rueful grin. 'The geese are keeping an eye on them. At least they're leaving the camera crew alone today. They're too busy guarding the newcomers.'

Caitlin smiled, seeing the geese gently nudging the puppies back on to the grass whenever they wandered near the edge of the lawn. They were just beginning to find their feet, but Daisy seemed happy to let the birds shepherd her flock while she simply lazed in the sunshine and gathered her strength. Thanks to good food and plenty of love and care, she was thriving, and her shaggy coat was beginning to take on a healthy glow.

The film crew spent some time working around the house and outbuildings, and then moved off to concentrate their attention on the wooded area around the smallholding. A couple of villagers acted as extras, wandering along the footpath that led from Brodie's property to the copse beyond. The same man who'd been wheezing the day before was there. Caitlin stood and watched them go.

'I think they've finished with us for now,' Brodie said as he walked with her to the back of her house. He gave her a long, appreciative look. 'It looks as though I have you all to myself at last.'

'Is that what you want?' she murmured.

'Oh yes,' he said. They came to a halt on the terrace overlooking the lawn and in the privacy of a jasmine-covered arbour he leaned towards her.

'I never seem to get you alone, what with David being around, the film crew and whoever else decides on a whim to drop by.' He slid his arm around her waist and tugged her towards him. 'You've had all sorts of creatures demanding your attention: a rabbit, the quail, Daisy and the pups, three terrifying geese— and for all I know a motherless kitten could turn up at any minute to distract you. I'm all for moving in on you while I can.'

She smiled and lifted her face to him, rewarded instantly when he bent his head to hers and claimed her lips. She was ready for his kiss, wanting it, needing it, craving the feel of his arms around her. He eased her against the rustic trellis, supporting her with his forearm, raining kisses over her cheek and throat, nuzzling the creamy velvet of her shoulder beneath the loose collar of her shirt. 'Do you think we could be

together, you and I?' he murmured. 'A couple? Could
we give it a go?'

The sweet fragrance of white jasmine filled the air
as she moved against him, pressing her soft curves into
his muscular frame. 'Oh, yes…yes.'

She heard his gasp, revelled in his strength, and
lost herself in his kisses, running her hands up over
his chest, delighting in the swift intake of his breath
as his body tautened against her.

'Ah, Caity…you've made me so happy. I want you so
badly. You know it, don't you?' His voice was rough-
ened, the words thick against her cheek, her lips.
'When I saw you first thing this morning, it took all
I had to keep my hands off you.' He kissed her again,
hungrily. 'You're so lovely, so perfect, Caity. You're
everything I could ever want.'

'Mmm… I want you too, Brodie,' she murmured.
She snuggled up against him, loving the way he needed
her, exhilarated by the feel of him, by the delicious
stroking of his hands as they moved over her curves,
filling her with feverish excitement. If only it was true,
what he was saying. Could she really be everything he
could ever want? 'I want you so much…'

She was seduced by him, by the heady perfume
of jasmine that wafted on the air, the warmth of the
sun on her bare arms and legs and by his wonderful,
coaxing hands that seemed to know instinctively how
to make her body yearn for more. Why shouldn't she
accept what he was offering, let him take her on that
tantalising, breathtaking voyage of discovery?

'Let's go inside the house…' His voice was husky,

urgent, ragged with passion; she was more than willing to go along with him.

'Okay.' She didn't want to break away from him and neither, it seemed, did he want to move away from her. He kept his arm around her as they walked the short distance to the kitchen door.

But before they made it as far as the kitchen, they heard David's voice calling to them from across the garden. 'Are you there, bro? I need to talk to you. Brodie?'

The geese started cackling at the intrusion and Caitlin gave a slow, heavy sigh, her fizzing, shooting senses coming back down to earth with a bump. Beside her, Brodie stiffened.

'One of these days...' Brodie said, gritting his teeth. 'He's my brother,' he said under his breath, 'and I'm very attached to him, but there are times, I swear, I could...' He didn't finish what he was saying.

David came around the back of the house. 'There you are. I thought I saw you both in the garden a minute ago. There's a problem with the look of the back of the house—your house, Brodie. It's too neat. The director wants to know if we can put some plants there in place of yours—shrubs and so on—to make it look straggly and overgrown. We'll put everything back how it was afterwards.'

'Sure. That's fine.' Brodie's answer was brisk and to the point. 'Why don't you go and see to it right away?'

'Hmm. Am I sensing something here?' David looked from one to the other. 'The thing is, I would go away...but you need to come and talk to the direc-

tor and see what he wants to do. There are papers you
need to sign.'

'You can sign them for me.' Brodie's impatience was
showing and David studied him thoughtfully.

'Sorry, no can do. Anyway, you did say you'd be
available to deal with any queries that came up today.'

His glance went to Caitlin, who was waiting edgily
through this back-and-forth chitchat. She was coming
to realise how very close she'd come to burning her
boats with Brodie.

'He seems anxious to be rid of me,' David commented. He raised his brows in a silent question that
she decided to ignore. 'I'm hugely jealous,' he said, his
dark eyes glinting with mischief. 'You know that, don't
you? You always said you wouldn't lose your heart to
either of us because we would trample all over it.'

'Leave it off, David,' Brodie warned, his whole
body tense. But David merely smiled, for all his worth
playing the part of the irritating younger brother. He
glanced at Caitlin, as though expecting an answer.

'Did I say that?' She sounded breathless, even to
her own ears. 'That was a long time ago.'

'Yes, well, nothing much has changed. Except I'm
the one you should go for.' Again, that imp of devilment
appeared in his eyes. 'I'd make you happy.'

'You're right,' she agreed. 'Nothing's changed, has
it? I ought to know better than to listen to either of
you. My father used to warn me about you two. "Pair
of young rascals," he said. "Full of testosterone, looking for conquests and moving on."'

She'd been very young when her father had died—

fifteen years old and emotionally insecure. But her father had loved and cherished her; she knew that. He'd wanted the best for her and she'd missed him so much after he died. Perhaps his loss was the reason she'd tried so hard not to fall for Brodie...then and now. It hurt so much to lose someone you loved. Was she making the biggest mistake of her life?

David smiled. 'Your father had a point. We were very young and immature.' He started to move away across the terrace. 'See you in a minute or two, bro.'

Caitlin turned to Brodie with a rueful smile. 'Perhaps you should go and sign your papers. I think that motherless kitten has arrived.'

'I guess he has.' Brodie gave her a long, steady look. 'Another time, then,' he said quietly. 'I've already waited a lifetime...what does a little longer matter?'

'I don't know about that, Brodie,' she said equally softly. 'I don't know if I'm making a mistake.'

'He was just teasing you.'

'I know. But perhaps it's a good thing that I have time to think. I've just finished one relationship. Maybe this is the wrong time to be stepping back into the fray.'

'And, then again, it might be the perfect time. Sometimes you need to follow your instincts.'

She nodded. 'Okay,' she said softly, still troubled.

'We'll be fine,' he said. 'I promise.' He gently brushed her mouth with his and then went off in the direction of the camera crew.

She watched him go, the memory of his kiss imprinted on her lips. David's comments played over in her mind, though. He had given her food for thought and taken her right back to when this had all started. Brodie had pursued her since they were teenagers. He'd never faltered, taking up where he'd left off as soon as they'd met up again. He couldn't resist a challenge.

Perhaps to him she was simply the one that got away and that was why he persisted in going after her.

CHAPTER SEVEN

CAITLIN WAS NEARING the end of her shift on Monday afternoon when the staff nurse asked her to look in on baby Olivia. 'Her mum's worried—she had her operation first thing this morning, and she started taking small feeds six hours later, but the poor little thing's still vomiting.'

'Okay, Cathy. Bless her—I'll go and see her now. She's still on a fluid drip until her full feeding regime is restored, so there aren't any worries on that score.'

She hurried away to go and look in on the mother and baby. She and Brodie had been busy all day and hadn't really had a chance to talk. Even at lunchtime he'd been involved in meetings with chiefs from the local health authority.

Now she went to see Olivia, checking the heart and respiration monitor, glad to find that all was well there. The infant looked reasonably content, squirming a little in her mother's arms; every now and again her pink rosebud mouth made little sucking movements.

'Hi,' Caitlin said, going to sit down beside them. 'I hear she's having a bit of a problem?'

'That's right.' The mother's brow creased with anxiety. 'She keeps being sick. Does it mean the operation hasn't worked?'

'Not at all. The surgeon reported that everything went very well. This type of surgery is very low risk.' She stroked the baby's palm and felt the infant's fingers close around hers. 'She's lovely, isn't she?' A quiver of unforeseen, overwhelming maternal instinct ran through her, melting her insides.

The mother nodded and smiled. 'Yes, she is. She's so precious to us and this is all very upsetting.'

'It *is* upsetting, but it's quite usual for a baby to be sick after this kind of surgery. It happens because there's often a bit of swelling after the operation, but that will soon go down and she should be able to feed normally after that. I'll ask the nurse to check how often she's being fed and how much, and to work with you on that. Things should soon settle. She just needs tiny feeds for the time being. I'm sure she'll be fine.'

'Thanks.' The girl looked relieved. 'I'm sorry to be such a pain…'

'No, you're not being a pain at all. I'm sure all new mums worry. It's natural.'

Maybe one day she would be holding her own child in her arms, looking down at him or her with such love and tenderness. She already knew how good Brodie was with children; she'd seen him in action with children and animals and he was wonderful with them all. Did he want to have a family of his own? Would he ever contemplate taking that step? She'd dearly love to have children with him. He'd be a fantastic father.

A rush of heat rippled through her. She'd never once contemplated having a family with Matt, even when they'd talked about getting engaged. It was very odd but it simply hadn't occurred to her.

She met up with Brodie as he was getting ready to leave the hospital for the day. 'They're filming at the village pub this evening,' he told her. 'David said he hoped we would both be there.'

'Yes, he mentioned it to me.'

'How do you feel about it? Do you fancy going along? We don't have to do anything—the camera crew will be filming the actors and we'll be in the background somewhere with the rest of the pub's customers.'

'Yes, okay. I'd like to go.'

He smiled. 'Good. It's a date, then. He said to come early—he wants me to meet someone, something to do with one of the photos that appeared in the papers. He says it's important, but he didn't go into details. I can't imagine what that's about.'

'Perhaps a talent scout saw you on camera and wants you to do a hero doctor drama series,' she said with a smile.

He laughed. 'Of course, why didn't I think of that?'

She walked with him to the car park and her expression sobered. 'Are you and David getting on all right now? I was a bit concerned after the way you were sniping at one another yesterday afternoon.'

'We're fine. It's just banter—on his part, especially.' He gave a wry smile. 'David was a demon for trying to wind me up when we were younger...you probably remember that?'

She nodded. 'He hasn't changed much, has he?' she said with a smile.

He shook his head, sending her a sidelong glance. 'Though I suspect yesterday's comments came about because he has a big crush on you.'

She shook her head. 'No, he doesn't. He may have fancied his chances years ago, but now it's all bravado—designed to get a response from you, I think. He only makes a play for me when you're around. That's a definite hangover from the old days.'

'Maybe.' They parted company as they reached their cars. 'I'll call for you in about an hour and a half,' he said. 'And we'll stroll down to the pub together...is that okay?'

She nodded. 'It's the last of the filming sessions today, isn't it? I heard they'd arranged a celebratory buffet meal for everyone in the lounge bar for when it's all over.'

'Sounds good to me.'

Caitlin rushed through her chores as soon as she arrived back at the house, feeding the animals and making sure Daisy and the pups had a run outside before quickly getting ready for the evening. She showered and dressed in slim-fit jeans and a layered top. Leaving her hair loose to flow in burnished chestnut curls to her shoulders, she applied a swift dab of make-up to her face, finishing off with a light spray of perfume.

Brodie sucked in his breath when he called for her a short time later. 'You look beautiful,' he said, his eyes darkening with appreciation. He stepped inside the house and moved towards her. 'Shall we give the pub a miss and stay in?'

'Behave yourself,' she admonished him with a laugh. 'Anyway, you know David will only come and find you if you don't turn up—or else the director will decide it's a good idea to do a final scene outside your house.'

'I don't care. I'm prepared to risk it,' he murmured, walking further into the hallway and sliding his arms around her. As an afterthought he pushed the front door shut with his foot to give them some privacy then he lowered his head and stole a kiss.

Instantly, in an intuitive, innate response, her lips softened beneath his and she kissed him tenderly, wanting him, loving him, yet at the same time warring with herself about what she was doing. It had hurt so badly to be rejected when she'd been with Matt; she couldn't help feeling she was storing up trouble for the future by getting ever more deeply involved with Brodie. The trouble was, she couldn't help herself.

Brodie deepened the kiss, tugging her closer to him so that she could feel the passion burning in him. There was no mistaking his desire for her. His hands moved over her, making sweeping forays over all the curves and planes of her body, shaping her, tantalising her with his gentle, knowing expertise; all the while his lips teased the softness of her mouth and made gentle trails over the silken skin of her throat.

His fingers slid beneath the flowing hem of her top, slowly gliding upwards until he found the soft swell of her silk-clad breasts and lingered there. A shuddery, satisfied sigh escaped him. 'Ah, Caity, you're so lovely...'

A muffled gasp caught in her throat. His touch was heavenly, sensual, luring her into a state of feverish euphoria. It was pure seduction, taking her to heights of ecstasy she'd never known before, making her want ever more. She groaned softly, heat intensifying inside her as he moved against her. She felt the brush of his thigh against hers, his hard, muscular body driving her to distraction.

And then came the jarring, insistent bleep of a mobile phone and she blinked in bewilderment, her body recoiling in a spasm of shock.

'What is it? Who can it be...?' She stared up at him, dazed, uncomprehending. Her whole being was in a state of traumatic distress.

He shook his head. Perhaps he managed to recover his equilibrium faster than she did because he said cautiously, 'It's not my phone. It must be yours.'

'Oh...are you sure?'

He nodded.

Befuddled, she searched in her jeans pocket with shaking hands and drew out her phone. It was the hospital calling and immediately she was on alert, worried. Was something wrong with her mother? Had she taken a turn for the worse?

She listened carefully to what the nurse had to say. 'Thank you. Thanks for letting me know,' she said quietly at last.

She cut the call and looked up at Brodie. 'My mother

can come home tomorrow—if her blood pressure, pulse and so on are okay. Her blood oxygen level is fine now, apparently. The consultant just paid her a quick visit while he was there to see another patient.' She gave a rueful smile. 'I think, actually, she probably badgered him into it.'

'That sounds like your mother—she likes to get things sorted. She must be feeling a lot better.'

She nodded, looking at him, not knowing quite what to say. The mood had been totally disrupted. Now that she was thinking clearly again, making love right now didn't seem like such a good idea. She might love him and want children with him but she wanted the whole package: love, marriage and a vow of eternal devotion. Was he even capable of that?

'I guess we ought to head for the pub,' he said reluctantly, gauging her reaction. 'I suppose you were right earlier. David's quite likely to come looking for me. He seemed particularly anxious for me to meet this person.'

'A man?'

'A woman, I believe.'

She frowned. 'Do I need to be jealous?'

'Would you be?' He sounded almost hopeful and that surprised her a little. Didn't he know how she felt about him?

'Oh yes, very much so. I want you all to myself.'

'Good. I'm glad about that.' He opened the door and she stepped out onto the porch with him.

'The trouble is, I never quite feel safe with you, Brodie…emotionally, I mean. I'm never sure if you'll decide to look around and see if the grass is greener somewhere else.'

They started to walk along the country lane. 'Have I ever given you any reason to doubt me?' he asked. 'Nowadays, I mean...since I came back here?' He studied her, his expression suddenly brooding. 'Surely I'm the one who needs to be on his guard? After all, you're still hankering after Matt, aren't you? How do I compete with him?'

She shook her head. 'You're wrong about that. I don't even think about him any more. It's over.'

He made a short, dismissive sound. 'I don't believe that's true. His name came up the other day when we were having lunch and your hands were shaking. I don't think you're over him at all.'

She sent him a troubled look. 'It was a shock, that's all: what he did; the way he finished with me... Everything in my life changed overnight. It was just a reaction to what had been a harrowing episode in my life.'

'Well, when you can be with him or think about him without trembling, maybe then I'll believe you. Till then, it's all up in the air.'

Caitlin pressed her lips together briefly. No matter what she said, she had the feeling he wouldn't believe her right now. Yet, deep inside, she truly wondered why she'd ever thought she was in love with Matt. He was a good man—pleasant company, supportive— but he'd never made her feel the way she did when she was with Brodie.

'You don't need to worry about Matt,' she said.

He reached for her, holding her briefly, his hands

cupping her arms. 'I want you, Caity. I want you all to myself, and I'll do whatever I can to drive him from your mind. I'll prove to you that I'm good enough for you, that I won't let you down.'

Brodie made her insides tingle with longing, he made her blood fizz with excitement, and he made her yearn for him when he wasn't around. If she explained that to him it would more than likely incite him to launch a full-scale, bone-melting sensual assault on her body and mind, no holds barred, right here in the lane. Much as she'd love that, she wasn't at all sure she could handle the consequences.

She loved everything about him: the way he helped out around the smallholding without a care; the way he was there for her before she even knew she needed him; even the way he accepted her for what she was, without wanting to change her.

'Ah, you made it. Good.' David looked pleased to see both of them when they walked into the pub's lounge bar and several of the villagers who were seated nearby or standing by the bar nodded acknowledgement. In the background the camera crew were setting up, getting ready for filming, and the actors were going over their scene in readiness.

'Heard you're doing good things up at the hospital,' one of the men at the bar said to Brodie. 'My sister's little girl had to stay there for a day or so—they were very impressed.'

'I'm glad to hear it, Frank. We aim to please.'

Frank Brennan had been one of Brodie's arch accusers way back when Brodie had been an annoying teenager. He'd been subjected to trespass and minor vandalism and he'd borne the brunt of Brodie's talents as a graffiti artist on his various outbuildings. Caitlin looked on and smiled at how things had turned full circle.

'Also heard you had the offer of another job in London,' Frank went on. Caitlin frowned at that, sending Brodie a quick, sharp glance. He returned her gaze fleetingly, looking slightly uncomfortable.

This was the first she'd heard about any forthcoming new job. If it was true, it meant Brodie had kept his cards very close to his chest, and it seemed as though all her fears were coming to fruition. She felt a painful, involuntary clenching of muscle in her abdomen. He wasn't going to be staying around, was he? He was prepared to go all out after her, make her care for him beyond reason, then he would calmly leave as though it didn't matter at all. Being with her was simply a ripple on a pool.

She looked at him once more. Perhaps it was just a rumour. Ought she not at least give him the benefit of the doubt?

Brodie sent Frank a quizzical glance. 'News travels fast around here. How did you come to know about it?'

He wasn't denying it, then. Caitlin let out a slow, fraught breath. Her nerves were in shreds.

'Through my father-in-law. He works in admin at the hospital. Said the bosses at the local health authority were well taken with the way you'd changed things and wanted you to do the same thing at one of the London hospitals.' He gave Brodie an assessing look. 'So, what are you thinking? Will you be taking them up on the offer?'

So that was why he'd been involved in meetings at lunchtime. They must have been discussing the new role and the opportunities it presented.

'I don't know yet, Frank,' Brodie said. 'I've only been at this hospital for a short time and the new contract isn't due to start for a few months. I'm still thinking about it.'

'Well, whatever you decide, from the sound of things you'll go far.' Frank laughed. 'I never thought I'd hear myself saying that.'

'Likewise.'

Brodie went to the bar and bought drinks, sending Caitlin a cautious glance as he handed her a glass of sparkling wine. 'I was going to tell you,' he said, reading her thoughts accurately. 'I was just waiting for the time to be right.'

'When would that have been, I wonder?' In the background, she was conscious of the filming taking place, but at least the cameras weren't pointed her way.

He shrugged awkwardly. 'I knew you would be concerned about me moving on—but the offer came out of the blue very recently and out of respect for the bosses I have to give it some thought.'

She was distressed, certainly, and she might have said more, but Brodie's father came and stood next to them, looking uneasy.

He nodded towards Caitlin and then turned his narrowed gaze on Brodie. 'I couldn't help hearing what you and Frank were saying. So you're thinking of going away again in a few months? You don't like to stay still, do you? You've only just come back here.' There was almost a hint of accusation in his tone.

'It's more that I like to feel I'm achieving something,' Brodie answered carefully. 'I didn't go looking for the job offer. They came to me with it.'

'You'd call it being headhunted, I suppose?' His father's manner was gruff.

'I suppose.' Brodie took a swallow of his drink. He sent his father an odd, questioning look. 'I didn't think you'd be bothered.'

Caitlin nudged him. Despite her unhappy mood right now she felt she ought to remind him of the conversation they'd had a while ago. 'Remember what we talked about?' she said in an undertone.

His father might well care more for Brodie than he liked to admit. He could be carrying a burden of guilt that he hid from everyone. She only hoped Brodie would cotton on to what she was getting at. 'You don't always see things the way others do,' she murmured.

'No, that's true.'

David decided to join in. 'If Brodie took the job in London he'd get to see more of me, most likely,' he said, giving an exaggerated smile and showing his teeth. 'What better reason could he have for going there?'

'Like I said, I haven't made a decision yet.' Brodie looked at Caitlin then back at his father. 'Anyway, if I did make up my mind to accept it, it's only an hour and a half by car. I could easily get back here, the same as David does.'

'Sure. I get back here often enough,' David agreed. He was about to expand on that when he saw someone heading towards the bar and excused himself. 'I have to go—I'll be back in a minute or two.'

Brodie's father shifted awkwardly. 'I know you well enough, Brodie. You'll do what you want, I don't doubt. You always did.' He turned away to take a long gulp from his drink; Frank Brennan took him to one side to talk to him about the repairs going on at Mill House.

'I hear you're thinking of having the roof fixed,' Frank said. 'I can match up the slates for you, if you want. I know they're special—a particular kind.'

Caitlin didn't hear Colin Driscoll's muffled reply. She was uneasy.

'An hour and a half may sound like nothing at all,' she told Brodie, 'But it's a three-hour commute in the day and he knows it wouldn't be too long before it turned into a long-distance relationship.' She blurted out what was on her mind then took refuge in sipping her drink.

'You're not just talking about my father and me, are you?' Brodie asked, his gaze moving over her curiously. 'You're thinking about the way it might affect our relationship—yours and mine?'

'It applies equally well to both—though, yes, I'm thinking about you and me. It's hopeless, though, isn't it? If you're planning on going away it looks as though it's even more unlikely that you and I will ever get together in any meaningful way, doesn't it?'

'You could always come with me.' His blue eyes were suddenly dark and impenetrable like the sea.

'Could I?' She looked at him and inside her heart wept. 'You don't really think that's a possibility, do you? You know I wouldn't want to be too far from Mum now that she's had a fall. I couldn't leave her to fend for herself. I'd always be worrying about her.'

Besides, it would take more than a casual offer of 'why don't you tag along with me?' to make her go with him, wouldn't it? Where was the love, the cherishing, the for-ever promise that she desperately needed?

'It doesn't have to be a major problem,' Brodie insisted. 'We could work something out.'

Her heart lurched at the prospect. Could they? Was it possible?

He took a step back from her as David came over to them, bringing with him an attractive girl who looked to be in her late twenties. Caitlin knew the chance of pursuing the conversation was lost for now, and she resigned herself to putting it on the back burner.

'This is the young woman I wanted you to meet.' David introduced the woman to both of them. 'This is Deanna.' To Deanna, he said, 'This lovely girl is Caitlin, and this is my brother, Brodie.'

Deanna smiled at both of them. She had mid-length dark hair and grey eyes; she looked at Brodie as though she was especially thrilled to be meeting him.

'I just had to come and see you,' she said, gazing up at him eagerly, her eyes shining. 'I saw your picture in the paper and I knew I had to get in touch with the film company.' She hesitated. 'I hope you don't mind?'

'I don't think I mind,' Brodie said, smiling at her enthusiasm. 'Is there any reason why I should?'

'It's this picture, you see.' She pulled a sheet of newspaper from her jacket pocket and opened it out. Brodie was in the picture, looking straight into the camera as he attempted to rescue the cameraman from the goose intent on pecking his leg.

'Okay…' he said slowly. 'That's me.' He looked at her questioningly.

'There's another picture you should see.' This time she opened up her handbag and carefully took out an envelope. 'Take a look at this.'

She waited with bated breath. Brodie gave her a puzzled look but opened up the envelope and drew out a glossy photograph. He stared at the photograph for several seconds and then looked back at Deanna. He passed the photo to Caitlin. When he spoke, his voice was cracked, almost a whisper, as though he was in shock.

'Who is this?' he asked.

Deanna pulled in a deep breath. 'He's my father,' she said. 'That photo was taken when he was a young man. When I put the two pictures together, I knew I had to come and find you. You're exactly alike, aren't you?'

Caitlin looked at the photo and sucked in her breath, her mind racing, while Brodie appeared to be struggling to find words. 'Is he…does he…does he know about me…about the picture in the paper?'

Deanna shook her head. 'He's not seen it yet. He's been busy lately—he had to go out to Sweden to sort out a new order for his company.' She glanced at her watch. 'He was flying back today—in fact he should have landed at the airport a couple of hours ago. Any-

way, I wanted to talk to you before I showed him.'
She hesitated. 'It's a bit awkward. He never mentioned
having a son—apart from my younger brother, Ben, I
mean. But there's such a strong likeness between the
two of you, I can't help thinking there's a connection
between you. I had to come and find out if there's any
history, any kind of background that we didn't know
about—'

She broke off, floundering a bit. 'Do you understand
what I'm trying to say? I don't know if my father had
a relationship with a woman before he met and married my mother, but if he did...I think you could be
my half-brother.'

Brodie dragged in a deep breath and Caitlin wanted
to wrap her arms around him and hug him. This must
be an incredible moment for him. Instead, being in a
public place, she reined in her instincts and contented
herself with sliding an arm around his waist, trying to
show him some silent, unobtrusive support.

He looked at her fleetingly and a wealth of under-
standing passed between them. Then he braced himself.

'You've obviously spoken to David, about this,' he
said, glancing at David for confirmation, then back to
Deanna. 'So you must know something of my background.' David acknowledged that with a slight move-
ment of his head.

'Yes, I have,' Deanna said excitedly. 'That's what
made me think there could be something in it. David
told me your mother's maiden name—I want to ask my

father if he ever knew her.' She looked at him search-ingly. 'How do you feel about that?'

Brodie was silent for a moment or two. Then he said guardedly, 'It depends... Obviously I want to know the truth, but I'm not sure how he might react, or whether his response is going to cause trouble for your family—for your mother and your brother. They're bound to have strong feelings about this—and in the end they might have more to lose than I do. I've always wanted to know who my father is but I don't want to cause heartache for his family.'

Deanna relaxed. 'My father's an easy-going kind of man, a very fair-minded person. And I've already sounded my mother out about any previous relation-ships. She said there was a woman in Dad's life before they were married but it was over when she met him.' She gave Brodie a steady, assessing look. 'I'd really like your permission to ask my father about this.'

Brodie exhaled slowly. 'You don't need my permis-sion. But you have it anyway. Go ahead and ask him.'

Deanna still seemed to have something on her mind. 'What is it?' Brodie asked.

'Um... I could phone him right now?' She said it in a questioning way.

Brodie nodded, taking a deep breath. 'Okay. Go ahead.'

'Perhaps it'll be better if I go outside, into the gar-den to make the call. Why don't you come with me? It will be quieter out there and we can find a more pri-vate place to call him.'

'Okay. But I want David and Caitlin to come along.'

'All right.'

Caitlin had been afraid she would be left out of this major event but her spirits soared when Brodie included her. He put his arm around her waist and led her to the paved seating area outside.

They sat at a bench table in a far corner, brightened by a golden pool of light that spilled out from an overhead lamp. Deanna phoned her father and, after chatting to him briefly about his trip abroad and his flight home, she told him about the item of news featured in the paper and gently sounded him out about his life before he met her mother.

'Did you ever know a woman called Sarah Marchant?' Deanna asked.

Caitlin didn't hear what he said but Deanna listened, glanced at Brodie and then said, 'So you were involved with her for a while?' The conversation continued and after a while Deanna said, 'Dad, I think there's something you should know…someone you should meet.'

It was a fairly lengthy conversation; when it eventually came to a close, Deanna put down her phone and looked at Brodie. 'He'd like to see you. He suggested that either he could come here or you could meet in London?'

Brodie gave it some thought. 'I'll go to London,' he said. 'After all, it isn't just my father I have to meet. It looks as though I have to catch up with a whole new family I knew nothing about until now.'

Deanna hugged him. 'I'm so glad I saw that picture in the paper,' she said. 'I can't describe to you what a shock it was. I was certain you must be related to me in some way.'

Brodie hugged her in return then after a few minutes they all trooped back into the bar. The filming was finished and the landlord was busy setting out the food the production company had asked him to provide.

It was a wonderful buffet, colourful, tasty and beautifully presented; Caitlin duly tucked in alongside Brodie, his brother and newfound half-sister. They were all in a happy mood, smiling and cheerful.

She couldn't help thinking, though, as she let Brodie tempt her with filo prawns with sweet chilli dip. and mozzarella and sunblush-tomato bruschetta, that this celebratory meal was the exact opposite of what she was feeling.

She didn't feel like making merry, because Brodie was going to London to meet his new family—what were the chances he would be tempted to stay there with them? He was more than keen to go and it didn't call for a lot of working out to know that the prospect of taking up a new job there would absolutely complete the picture for him.

'I could go over there next weekend,' Brodie said to her, smiling as he helped himself to a selection from the cheese board. 'Will you come with me?'

'I'd love to,' she said, but frowned, thinking about the practicalities. 'But I don't know if I should leave Mum alone so soon after she's home from hospital. And there are the animals to see to: she won't be up to it for quite a while, with her mobility problems. It'll be some time before she's walking unaided.'

'I'm sure we could find somebody to help out, if only for a short time.'

'I suppose so,' she agreed. 'She has friends in the village who would be glad to help.'

'But something else is bothering you, isn't it?' He studied her, his gaze shifting over her thoughtfully. 'I can read you, Caitlin. What is it?'

'Nothing.' She smiled at him, not wanting to spoil the moment for him. 'I'm really, really happy for you, Brodie. This is what you've wanted for so many years and it's wonderful that you have the chance of some kind of closure.'

'But? There is a *but*, isn't there?'

Clearly, he wasn't going to leave it alone. She lifted her hands in a helpless gesture.

'I'm just worried about how things will work out in the long term—for us, I mean. I can see you wanting to move away now that you've found your family. It's natural you'll want to be with them and, with the job offer, how could it have worked out better? It's bound to affect us, though.'

She looked at him unhappily, taking in a deep breath. 'I want to be with you, Brodie, but I came back to Ashley Vale to make my home here—I don't think I want to uproot myself again.'

He frowned. 'The truth is, you came back here because Matt was getting married to Jenny.'

'Initially, that was the reason, yes, but then things changed. My mother had an accident. That made things different.' He had her on the defensive now and she didn't like it. She was confused—about him, about everything. Her emotions were tangled and for the life of her she couldn't sift her way through them.

'Are you putting up excuses, Caitlin? Don't you want to be with me?' His dark eyes narrowed. 'I can't help thinking I was right all along, that you can't make up your mind to be with me because you're not over Matt yet. You can't move on. There won't be any future for you and me while he's there between us, will there?'

His jaw clenched. 'Maybe I should take up this offer of a job and give you time to decide what you really do want?'

'Are you trying to make me choose?' Her voice broke and she looked at him with tears shimmering in her eyes. 'Matt doesn't come into it. He never did, where you were concerned. I always cared for you, but you weren't around, Brodie. What was I supposed to do? You left. You stayed away for years. And now you want me to choose between going away from here or staying—between being with you or losing you.'

She gulped in a quick breath. 'I don't want to choose, Brodie, and I don't want to persuade you to do something against your best interests. You're the one who has to decide. Stay or go.' She pressed her lips together briefly to stop them from trembling. 'I've made my decision, for good or bad, and I'll live with it.'

CHAPTER EIGHT

'How did you get on in London this weekend?' Cathy was keen to know how Brodie and Caitlin had fared when he'd gone to meet his father for the first time.

'It went well, on the whole,' Caitlin answered. 'But I think Brodie found it all a bit strange.' As she finished writing up the prescription for Jason's medication, she glanced across the desk at the nurse. 'He said he didn't expect to feel quite the way he did. It was a bit overwhelming.'

'I can imagine it would be. After all, from what I've heard, his natural father is a complete stranger to him. He didn't know anything about him, his life or his relationship with his mother. Brodie said it was like a bolt from the blue, learning that he was around and that he wanted to meet him.'

Caitlin nodded, handing her the prescription. Young Jason was finally being discharged from hospital today and the medication was to tide him over until his GP saw him next. The little boy was doing really well now, gaining in strength every day. She was glad to see him going home but she would miss him, she acknowledged. Sammy too, was being allowed home on a new regime of medication to help strengthen his bones. He was another one she would miss—he'd started to come out of his shell and was a favourite with all the staff.

'It's true,' she said now, thinking about Brodie and his new family. 'He didn't know they existed. I'm not sure what he expected, really, going to see them... I don't think he knew himself what might come of it but for a first meeting it turned out better than he imagined. We met his father in a pub to start with, so that we could talk in private.'

His natural father had been astonished to find that he had a son he knew nothing about. Brodie's mother had apparently said nothing to him, probably thinking he wouldn't want to know, but he was horrified to learn that she'd kept her pregnancy to herself. He would have stood by her and his son, he'd said.

But Caitlin didn't say any of that to Cathy. It seemed too private, too personal, and it was up to Brodie if he wanted to share that with anyone else. 'Anyway, then he took us to his house and we had a meal together— the whole extended family. It was...surreal.'

They'd all got on well together. His half-brother and half-sister especially had encouraged him to accept the promotion he'd been offered and go to live closer to them so they could keep in touch regularly. Even so, Caitlin still didn't know what he planned to do.

He seemed to be keeping his options open and, much as she longed for him to stay here in Ashley Vale with her, she couldn't blame him for looking further afield. He'd always worked hard to succeed—everything he did was designed to further his career—and it looked as though his efforts were paying dividends.

'Are we ready for the little girl?' Brodie strode briskly into the children's unit and checked his watch. A twelve-month-old girl was being brought in from the hospital where Caitlin used to work for specialist treatment. 'She'll be here in about ten minutes.'

Caitlin nodded. 'We're all set.' Cathy left them, hurrying over to the pharmacy to get Jason's prescription filled.

'Good. I want this transfer to go smoothly. If it all goes well she'll be able to have the operation tomorrow morning.' He glanced at her, his dark eyes brooding. 'Are you okay with everything? You're prepared?'

'You mean because it's Matt who's bringing her here?'

'Yes, that's what I mean.' His tone was unusually curt.

'Of course. You don't need to worry, Brodie, I'll be fine.' She frowned. 'Look, I know you must have things you need to do, meetings to go to and so on... You can leave everything to me. There won't be a problem. Matt and I are both professionals, after all.'

'Hmm.' His mouth flattened. 'That isn't exactly what's bothering me. I think you know that.'

'I told you, I'm over him.' She didn't try to argue the point any more. This was a difficult time for Brodie, she recognised that; if he was unusually tense right now it was probably to be expected. His mood wouldn't have darkened simply because of Matt's impending arrival, would it? Matt was his friend and they kept in fairly regular contact with one another. They must have smoothed things over with one another by now.

No, his taut, preoccupied manner surely had more to do with discovering the existence of his real father after all these years of believing it would never happen. It had been a profound experience for him and it was bound to be unsettling.

For now, whatever state their emotions were in, they had to put all that to one side and concentrate on their work. The tot who would be arriving here any minute now had been suffering from symptoms of chest pain, bouts of fainting and shortness of breath. After specialised tests she'd been diagnosed with a narrowing of the pulmonary valve in her heart. This narrowing was causing a problem with the flow of blood to her lungs.

'They're here.' Caitlin heard the faint clatter of a trolley and hurried to meet her new small patient. Greeting Matt with a brief nod, she concentrated her attention on the baby. Connected up to various monitors that recorded her heart rhythm, respiration and blood oxygen, she was wheeled in to the ward and between them Caitlin, Brodie and Matt set about transferring the child to her new temporary home. She was a tiny, vulnerable little thing, and Caitlin wanted to pick her up and cuddle her. 'Hello, Emily,' she said softly. 'We're going to look after you now. We'll make sure you're going to be absolutely fine.'

'Her parents followed us here,' Matt said. 'They should arrive within a few minutes.'

Brodie nodded, acknowledging his friend and listening as he outlined her condition. 'We'll do what we can to get her settled and then I'll go and talk to the parents. It's a straightforward procedure she'll undergo tomorrow, a balloon valvuloplasty; she should be fine afterwards.'

Matt agreed. This hospital was a centre of excellence for catheterisation procedures; if everything went well and her vital signs were satisfactory the little girl would have treatment to widen the valve. Afterwards she should be able to live a normal life. There wouldn't even be much of a scar, because the catheter would be inserted in a vein at the top of the infant's leg and the thin tube would then be passed up to the heart. Once there, a balloon would be inflated to widen the valve. When that was done to the surgeon's satisfaction, the balloon would be deflated and would be removed along with the tube.

Brodie supervised the infant's admission to hospital but, once Caitlin had sorted out the baby's medication, he left the ward and went in search of the parents.

Caitlin saw him glance back once briefly in her direction—that same dark, brooding look in his eyes that she'd seen earlier—but then he continued swiftly on his way. It occurred to her at that moment that she hadn't realised quite how much Brodie kept his feelings locked up inside him. Perhaps the relationship she'd shared with Matt was one more seed of doubt that made him feel unworthy in some way. Maybe she ought to try to do something to get him to open up to her more.

'I heard your mother was back home after the problems with her hip and the emboli in her lungs,' Matt said, walking with her to the cafeteria a short time later. The paramedics who had accompanied the child were in there, taking a break before the journey home. 'How is she?'

'She's feeling much better, thanks.' Caitlin smiled, amazed at how relaxed she was in his company. 'She's using crutches to get about at the moment, and she has physiotherapy every day, but she seems to be doing very well. She's determined to get out and about to see to the animals and so on, so at the moment I'm having to make sure she doesn't overdo things. Of course, the puppies keep us on our toes. They're into everything.'

'I heard about the new additions to the menagerie. She'll be in her element.'

'Oh yes, she is. She's even contemplating keeping a couple of the puppies, though we've managed to find people who want to take care of them when they're old enough to leave their mother.'

'Well, if she's taking a keen interest in things it sounds as though she's going to be all right in the long run. We were worried when she didn't make it to the wedding.'

Caitlin nodded. She expected to feel a pang of dismay at the mention of the big event, but nothing happened, and she felt an immense lightening of her spirits. 'Yes, it was difficult for her.' She glanced at him. 'I thought it all went off very well.'

'Yes, it did.' He bought two coffees and a couple of buns and started to carry the tray over to the table where the paramedics were seated. 'I'm glad you came along on the day,' he told her as they walked across the room. 'I was worried about you. I know I treated you badly…but things just sort of slid out of my control.'

'I know. It doesn't matter. Forget about it.'

'Are you sure?' He studied her, his expression solemn. 'Do you forgive me?'

'I do. It's all water under the bridge. I hope you and Jenny will be very happy together.' She meant it. It was as though a weight had been lifted off her.

He smiled. 'Thanks, Caity. I think I needed to hear you say that.' He pulled out a chair for her and said quietly, 'Brodie's been telling me what a fool I've been and how badly I treated you. I knew it, of course. I hated what I was doing to you and I hated that it was ruining my friendship with Brodie.'

'He's had a lot on his mind this last week or so. I wouldn't worry about it too much.'

'I don't know about that. He seems okay, but he's had a problem with me for quite some time. It just got worse recently.'

She frowned. 'I think he was jealous at first because you were with me, and then he was worried because he thought I was hurt.'

He nodded. 'I thought it might be something like that.'

She smiled as they approached the table. 'You've always been good friends. I'm sure things will be fine between you from now on.'

They sat opposite one another and chatted for a while, sharing the conversation with the paramedics, who were already well acquainted with Caitlin from her time at St Luke's.

After a while, Caitlin's pager bleeped and she made her apologies. 'I have to go and check up on a patient,' she said. 'I'm sure I'll see you all again before too long. Take care.'

She hurried along to the ward to look in on the youngster who had some time ago suffered an allergic reaction to penicillin. 'How are you doing, Janine?' she asked the five-year-old. 'Nurse tells me you've been feeling a bit breathless?'

Janine nodded. 'My chest feels a bit tight.'

'Okay, sweetheart. I'll have a listen, shall I?' Caitlin ran her stethoscope over the little girl's chest then went over to the computer at the desk and brought up her recent X-rays on the screen. They'd been done that morning to see if the infection was clearing.

'I think we'll give you some extra medicine,' she said, returning to the child's bedside after a while. 'Something you can breathe in to make your chest feel better.'

'All right.' The girl settled back against her pillows while the nurse went to sort out the new medication.

Brodie met Caitlin at the entrance to the patients' bay. 'Is there a problem?' he asked.

'It looks as though she has a bit of scarring on the lungs from the recent infection. I'll ask the physio to come and show her how to clear her chest and do breathing exercises. As long as she has antibiotic treatment for recurrent infections she should be okay.'

He nodded. 'So how did it go with Matt?' he asked. 'I thought you might still be with him, catching up on things.'

'No, I left him in the cafeteria when I was bleeped. Haven't you spoken to him?' She was surprised. 'I'd have thought he would have caught up with you again before he left.'

'I'm sure he will but he's not likely to tell me how he left things with you, is he?'

'Things are the same as they ever were,' she told him. Her gaze was thoughtful. His self-doubt was coming to the fore once again. 'I think you worry too much. He's married now and he only has eyes for Jenny. But you know that, don't you?'

'It's your feelings towards him that concern me,' he answered, but his pager bleeped before he had time to say any more. He checked the text message and immediately became businesslike. 'I have to go and assess a new patient.'

'Okay.' It was nearing the end of her shift and she said quickly, 'Will I see you back at the house tonight? You could come to supper if you like?'

He frowned. 'Thanks but I'm not sure if I can make it—I promised Dad I'd go and see him at Mill House. He seems to be anxious to put things on a better footing between us lately.' He lifted a dark brow. 'I guess you were right about him all along. He's fighting his own demons.'

She was disappointed she wouldn't be seeing him but she tried not to let it show. If he'd wanted to spend time with her, he would have found a way, wouldn't he? 'That's fine,' she said, trying to inject a note of nonchalance into her voice. 'I'm glad you and he are getting on better. When all's said and done, he's the one who brought you up. There must have been good times as well as bad.'

'Yes, there were. I think my memories were coloured by the way I found out he wasn't my real father and by the way he acted towards me when Mum died. He was angry and then he shut me out. I suppose that spurred me on to rebel against him all the more. We were both hurting and we lashed out at one another.'

She reached out and lightly touched his arm. 'I hope you can work things out between you.'

He made a wry face. 'I think we will. We're both up for it, now that we've finally squared up to the truth and realised our shortcomings.'

'Good luck, then.'

'Thanks, Caity.'

Caitlin finished her shift, checking on all her young charges and making sure they were comfortable and happy before she left the hospital.

Then she drove home, taking a route through town and along the country lanes, letting the quiet beauty of the Chilterns soothe her. She wanted to spend time with Brodie but, if he preferred to stay away, what could she do? Maybe she would have to get used to the idea that he wouldn't be around for much longer. David had already gone back to London. Was Brodie planning on joining him there in a few months' time?

'Sorry to love you and leave you, Caitlin,' her mother said shortly after she arrived home. A car horn sounded outside on the drive. 'My friend's arrived to take me to the book club meeting—did you remember it was on for tonight?'

'I remembered, Mum. Enjoy yourself.'

'I will. You'll get yourself something to eat, won't you? Because I'll be eating at Freda's house. There's the makings of a ploughman's lunch in the fridge and I made a batch of scones earlier. You could have them with some of that strawberry preserve.'

'Thanks, Mum. Don't worry about me. I'll have a shower and change and then I'll sort something out.'

'Good.' Her mother looked at her closely. 'You're looking a bit peaky. I hope you're not coming down with something.'

'I'm fine, really.'

'Hmm.' Her mother wasn't convinced. 'Is it Brodie? Is he the problem?' She frowned. 'I wish you and he could sort yourselves out. I thought when he bought the house next door he was all for settling down—but now that's all up in the air again with this job in London on the cards.'

Caitlin flicked her a glance. 'He told you about it?'

'Oh, yes. He said it's a fantastic opportunity. They've told him he can have carte blanche to make changes and there's even an executive house that goes with the job.'

Caitlin's heart sank. It sounded too good to be true and he was obviously impressed with the terms of the contract. Why would he even think of turning it down?

After her mother left with her friend, Caitlin showered and changed into jeans and a fresh, pretty top, then took Daisy for a walk along the quiet lane by the house. The terrier was happy to be out and about, fully restored to health with a shining, shaggy coat. She explored the grass verges, her tail wagging the whole time. Caitlin let her sniff and forage for a while, until finally she said, 'Come on, then, Daisy. It's time we were heading for home. I expect the puppies will be wanting their mum back.'

Daisy eagerly started back along the lane. She was unusually happy to hurry home and Caitlin had no idea what had brought about that enthusiasm until they rounded a bend in the road and saw a lone figure up ahead. He was coming towards them.

'Brodie?' Caitlin's eyes widened. 'I thought you'd be up at Mill House.'

He walked towards her, long and lean; his body was supple, his legs clad in dark chinos, his shirt open at the collar. 'Hi there. Yes, I was. I talked to Dad for a while and then told him I had an invitation for supper at your place. He seemed to think I should take you up on it.'

'And you were okay with that?'

'Oh, yes. I told him I was hoping he'd say that.'

She laughed, letting Daisy off the lead now that they were close to home. 'You got on well with him, then?'

'Yes, it was good. I think we smoothed a lot of things out. We'll be okay.'

The dog ran up to him, fussing around him delightedly, rapturous at finding her favourite person in all the world so near at hand, and Brodie stroked her silky head in return. 'I thought I'd find you both out on a walk along here,' he said.

'Mum's out at her book club meeting and I haven't started supper yet,' Caitlin told him. 'I thought I might make a pizza. What do you think?'

'Sounds good to me. I'll prepare the topping if you want to do the base?'

She nodded. 'Fair enough. There's cheese and ham and sun-dried tomatoes. Does that sound all right to you?'

'Perfect.'

They went into the house together. Daisy went off to find her offspring while Caitlin washed her hands at the sink and started to get organised for supper. She sent Brodie a quick glance. 'Did you catch up with Matt at the hospital before he left? I wondered if you and he had a chance to talk?'

She switched on the oven to warm and then gathered together the ingredients for the pizza, setting them out on the kitchen table. 'He seemed to think you had a problem with him.'

'So he said. Yes, we talked, for a short time. We're all right.' He started to chop ham and then grated the cheese she had put out on a board. 'I guess I just need to get over the fact that he dated you for what seemed like for ever.'

Her brow creased. 'That seems to have bothered you quite a bit.'

'It did. A lot.'

She shook her head. 'I'm sorry but I don't really understand.' She paused in the middle of putting together the mix for the pizza base. 'That all started a long while ago—Matt and me. Why would it worry you? You weren't around.'

He pulled a face. 'Maybe…but I wanted to be.'

She'd started to roll out the pizza base but now she

hesitated once more. 'I don't think I follow what you're trying to say.'

He moved his shoulders awkwardly. 'That's probably because I'm finding it hard to say it. I'm not used to baring my soul, Caity, but I suppose it's about time we had this out in the open.' He started to pace around the kitchen.

She frowned. 'Okay.' She spread sun-dried tomato paste over the pizza base and added the grated cheese and ham. 'What is it you need to tell me?' She slid the pizza into the oven and set the timer. 'Perhaps you should stand still and tell me before I get dizzy from watching you walking around.'

He gave a rueful smile at that but stood still. 'I always thought there was something missing in my life, something I was searching for. I thought I felt that way because I didn't know who my father was. I couldn't settle. I thought if I found him, found my natural father and discovered who I really was, that would resolve everything. But then I realised that wasn't the problem at all.'

'It wasn't?'

'No.' He shook his head. 'You see, it was you I wanted, Caity. It was you I wanted all along. You were the one who was missing from my life. I wanted you when we were teenagers but you weren't having any of it… I went away thinking I'd get over you, I'd make a new start…but it didn't happen. I never found anyone who could make me happy.'

He drew in a long breath. 'For a long time, I thought I didn't deserve to be happy. I believed I couldn't make you happy. Back when we were teenagers I wasn't good enough for you... I was so confused and out of sorts. I spent years thinking I wasn't good enough, that I was lacking in some way, not to be trusted. And then I heard you were with Matt and I knew I had to make one last effort to see you again, to see if things might change.'

He started to pace again and Caitlin stared at him, not daring to believe what he was saying.

'Is it true, Brodie? Do you mean it?'

He came over to her and wrapped his arms around her. 'It's definitely true, Caity. I came back here to Ashley Vale for one reason and one reason only. I wanted to be near you. I knew you would come to stay with your mother from time to time, so at least I would see you.'

He frowned. 'Knowing you and Matt were together drove me crazy. I'm ashamed to say I wanted to break things up between you. I couldn't stand the thought of you and him being together. In fact, I didn't want to think of you being with anyone other than me.'

'But you didn't say any of this to me.' She looked up at him, hardly daring to believe him, yet inside her heart was soaring. He'd missed her, he wanted to be with her and he'd come back to Ashley Vale to be near her.

She lifted her hand to his cheek, tracing the line of his strong jaw with the tips of her fingers. 'Why didn't you tell me?'

'How could I, when you seemed to be so much in love with Matt?' He bent his head and rested his cheek against hers. 'I'm sorry, but I was glad when you broke up with him. I thought maybe, in time, you'd come to see me in a different light, that you might come to love me as I love you.'

'Do you…love me?'

'I love you, Caity, more than anything. Being with you since I came back here just confirmed what I believed all along: that you're the only woman for me; my soulmate; my true love.' He held her close and kissed her and she clung to him, hardly able to breathe because she was so full of joy and love for him.

After a while, he reluctantly broke off the kiss to say raggedly, 'When you said you were unhappy because I left Ashley Vale, that you turned to Matt because I wasn't around, I began to hope there was a chance for you and me to be together. I hoped I could prove to you that I'm strong now, that I'm capable of true, heartfelt love, and that I can give you what you need. Tell me I'm right, Caity.'

'Brodie, I love you. I've known it for a long time now.' She kissed him fiercely, passionately, wanting to show him how much she cared for him.

'I think I turned to Matt because he was safe—he was steady and responsible—but as soon as you came back here I knew I'd made a huge mistake. I was in such a state of turmoil. I never felt for him, or for any man, what I feel for you. I always hankered after you but I was afraid to act on my feelings. I was so scared of being hurt, of loving you and losing you. Can you understand that? I think it all goes back to when I lost my father. It was so painful—I didn't want to risk you not loving me in return.'

'Ah, Caity...' He kissed her tenderly, his mouth ach-ingly sweet as he explored the softness of her lips. 'I love you and I'll never let you down. I want you to know that. I'll always be here for you. All you have to do is say you'll marry me—say the word and ev-erything will work out fine. We'll stay here and look after your mother and they can find someone else to take the job in London. It's not important. You're what matters to me, more than anything. I want you to know that you mean everything to me.' He gazed at her, his eyes dark with passion. 'Say you'll marry me, Caity?'

'Yes, Brodie. Yes. Yes, I will.' She was laugh-ing now with happiness, brimming over with it, still hardly daring to believe this was happening. Was it all a dream? Would she wake up and find it was a fanci-ful, wonderful fantasy?

But then the buzzer from the oven rang out, signal-ling that the pizza was cooked, an all too real sign that she was well and truly awake, and that someone would have to do something about it. Then they were both laughing, wrapped up in each other's arms, kissing and hugging, neither one wanting to let go of the other.

Daisy came in from the utility room to see what the noise was all about. She gave a short bark and nudged Brodie's leg.

'I think she wants me to stop the buzzer and get the pizza,' he said with a smile. 'You can tell who's going to be the boss in our house, can't you? A small, raggedy-haired dog with a tail that wags ten to the dozen.'

'"Our house",' Caitlin repeated with a smile. 'I love the sound of that.'

Brodie switched off the alarm and kissed her again, tenderly, thoroughly. 'So do I. Our house—a family home filled with love. Maybe even, some day, if you want it too, our own small brood of children.' He gazed down at her, holding her close.

'Oh, I do,' she murmured. 'It sounds absolutely perfect.'

* * * * *

MILLS & BOON®
Hardback – August 2015

ROMANCE

The Greek Demands His Heir	Lynne Graham
The Sinner's Marriage Redemption	Annie West
His Sicilian Cinderella	Carol Marinelli
Captivated by the Greek	Julia James
The Perfect Cazorla Wife	Michelle Smart
Claimed for His Duty	Tara Pammi
The Marakaios Baby	Kate Hewitt
Billionaire's Ultimate Acquisition	Melanie Milburne
Return of the Italian Tycoon	Jennifer Faye
His Unforgettable Fiancée	Teresa Carpenter
Hired by the Brooding Billionaire	Kandy Shepherd
A Will, a Wish...a Proposal	Jessica Gilmore
Hot Doc from Her Past	Tina Beckett
Surgeons, Rivals...Lovers	Amalie Berlin
Best Friend to Perfect Bride	Jennifer Taylor
Resisting Her Rebel Doc	Joanna Neil
A Baby to Bind Them	Susanne Hampton
Doctor...to Duchess?	Annie O'Neil
Second Chance with the Billionaire	Janice Maynard
Having Her Boss's Baby	Maureen Child

MILLS & BOON®
Large Print – August 2015

ROMANCE

The Billionaire's Bridal Bargain	Lynne Graham
At the Brazilian's Command	Susan Stephens
Carrying the Greek's Heir	Sharon Kendrick
The Sheikh's Princess Bride	Annie West
His Diamond of Convenience	Maisey Yates
Olivero's Outrageous Proposal	Kate Walker
The Italian's Deal for I Do	Jennifer Hayward
The Millionaire and the Maid	Michelle Douglas
Expecting the Earl's Baby	Jessica Gilmore
Best Man for the Bridesmaid	Jennifer Faye
It Started at a Wedding...	Kate Hardy

HISTORICAL

A Ring from a Marquess	Christine Merrill
Bound by Duty	Diane Gaston
From Wallflower to Countess	Janice Preston
Stolen by the Highlander	Terri Brisbin
Enslaved by the Viking	Harper St. George

MEDICAL

A Date with Her Valentine Doc	Melanie Milburne
It Happened in Paris...	Robin Gianna
The Sheikh Doctor's Bride	Meredith Webber
Temptation in Paradise	Joanna Neil
A Baby to Heal Their Hearts	Kate Hardy
The Surgeon's Baby Secret	Amber McKenzie

0715 GEN STD LP

MILLS & BOON®
Hardback – September 2015

ROMANCE

The Greek Commands His Mistress	Lynne Graham
A Pawn in the Playboy's Game	Cathy Williams
Bound to the Warrior King	Maisey Yates
Her Nine Month Confession	Kim Lawrence
Traded to the Desert Sheikh	Caitlin Crews
A Bride Worth Millions	Chantelle Shaw
Vows of Revenge	Dani Collins
From One Night to Wife	Rachael Thomas
Reunited by a Baby Secret	Michelle Douglas
A Wedding for the Greek Tycoon	Rebecca Winters
Beauty & Her Billionaire Boss	Barbara Wallace
Newborn on Her Doorstep	Ellie Darkins
Falling at the Surgeon's Feet	Lucy Ryder
One Night in New York	Amy Ruttan
Daredevil, Doctor...Husband?	Alison Roberts
The Doctor She'd Never Forget	Annie Claydon
Reunited...in Paris!	Sue MacKay
French Fling to Forever	Karin Baine
Claimed	Tracy Wolff
Maid for a Magnate	Jules Bennett

MILLS & BOON®
Large Print – September 2015

ROMANCE

The Sheikh's Secret Babies	Lynne Graham
The Sins of Sebastian Rey-Defoe	Kim Lawrence
At Her Boss's Pleasure	Cathy Williams
Captive of Kadar	Trish Morey
The Marakaios Marriage	Kate Hewitt
Craving Her Enemy's Touch	Rachael Thomas
The Greek's Pregnant Bride	Michelle Smart
The Pregnancy Secret	Cara Colter
A Bride for the Runaway Groom	Scarlet Wilson
The Wedding Planner and the CEO	Alison Roberts
Bound by a Baby Bump	Ellie Darkins

HISTORICAL

A Lady for Lord Randall	Sarah Mallory
The Husband Season	Mary Nichols
The Rake to Reveal Her	Julia Justiss
A Dance with Danger	Jeannie Lin
Lucy Lane and the Lieutenant	Helen Dickson

MEDICAL

Baby Twins to Bind Them	Carol Marinelli
The Firefighter to Heal Her Heart	Annie O'Neil
Tortured by Her Touch	Dianne Drake
It Happened in Vegas	Amy Ruttan
The Family She Needs	Sue MacKay
A Father for Poppy	Abigail Gordon

MILLS & BOON®

Why shop at millsandboon.co.uk?

Each year, thousands of romance readers find their perfect read at millsandboon.co.uk. That's because we're passionate about bringing you the very best romantic fiction. Here are some of the advantages of shopping at www.millsandboon.co.uk:

* **Get new books first**—you'll be able to buy your favourite books one month before they hit the shops

* **Get exclusive discounts**—you'll also be able to buy our specially created monthly collections, with up to 50% off the RRP

* **Find your favourite authors**—latest news, interviews and new releases for all your favourite authors and series on our website, plus ideas for what to try next

* **Join in**—once you've bought your favourite books, don't forget to register with us to rate, review and join in the discussions

Visit **www.millsandboon.co.uk** for all this and more today!